TOWARD
AMNESIA

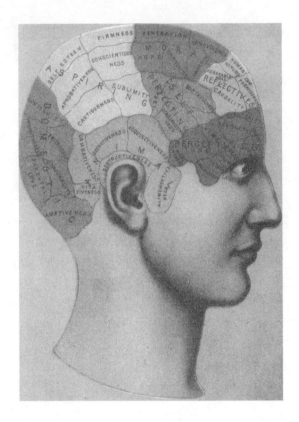

TOWARD
AMNESIA

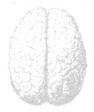

S A R A H
V A N   A R S D A L E

Riverhead Books
New York
1995

for Fred

RIVERHEAD BOOKS
a division of G. P. Putnam's Sons
Publishers Since 1838
200 Madison Avenue
New York, NY 10016

Library of Congress Cataloging-in-Publication Data

Van Arsdale, Sarah
Toward amnesia / by Sarah Van Arsdale.
p.   cm.
ISBN 1-57322-017-5
I. Title.
PS3551.R725T69   1995   95-10128 CIP
813'.54—dc20

Book design by Claire Naylon Vaccaro
Frontispiece courtesy of Nick and Luella Vaccaro

Printed in the United States of America

1   3   5   7   9   10   8   6   4   2

This book is printed on acid-free paper. ∞

I am grateful to the
following people for helping
to occasion this book: Judy
LeBold, Alison Bechdel,
Rachel Morton, Dr. Jules
Leavitt, Dr. Chris Wellins,
members of the Valley
Lesbian Writers Group and
the Buell Street Writers
Group, and my editor, Mary
South.

Thanks also to my
parents for their steadfast
encouragement.

Then practice losing farther, losing faster:
places, and names, and where it was you meant
to travel. None of these will bring disaster...

—Even losing you (the joking voice, a gesture
I love) I shan't have lied. It's evident
the art of losing's not too hard to master
though it may look like (*Write* it!) like disaster.

—ELIZABETH BISHOP
from "One Art"

TOWARD AMNESIA

It was on Memorial Day that I decided to achieve amnesia.

I knew this might require a tremendous amount of patience, so I started small. I put on an old pair of sunglasses, one of the few pairs I hadn't lost by last summer's end.

One pair dropped irretrievably into the water of Blue Lake up in Minnesota, when Libby and I paddled the canoe at daybreak through the tangled lilies. We were astonished that morning first to hear, and then to see, a huge living moose rise from the depths, all fur and rack and legs, dripping lake water and reeds like some prehistoric therapsid.

We were often astonished in each other's presence.

Another pair, I know, must have sunk into the depths of the dune grass of Okracoke where Libby and I had made love on her plaid blanket, our sweatshirts soft against our breasts, my weight on her ridging deep striations into the sand, the late-afternoon air cooling our faces and bare legs.

All the other sunglasses just disappeared: I'd lift my keys from the hallway table, reach for my shades, and there'd just be a roll of Libby's film and the telephone bill lying next to the vase of irises. Or I'd push them onto my forehead to read a road map, then reach up again, and I'd be brushing my hand through my long empty hair. Gone. Gone to some parallel universe notched out in the fissures between those atoms by which we swear.

I was very sensitive to light.

The biggest drawback to my one remaining pair of sunglasses actually turned to my advantage, as happens with some things in life—typographical errors, or a robbery you're insured against. These shades were very dark, and had the effect of blanking out my eyes and cheekbones to anyone bothering to look at me, and from behind them, the world appeared on the verge of plunging headlong into night.

I'd gotten them on one of our beach trips when, nearly there, our towels and books and binoculars piled in the back seat of Libby's Land Rover, I'd reached into the straw bag at my feet and patted around: my new book, *Sense Receptors in Ectoskeletals;* my extra t-shirt; my wallet and comb and a bottle of suntan lotion; my jar of Noxzema; a couple of Hershey's Kisses; and no sunglasses.

I rifled through the bag again.

"Did another pair take off?" Libby asked, knowing what was missing without even looking down from the road. "They're starting a fan club for you, wherever they are."

"Terrific. I wish they'd open a chapter on Earth. Could we stop at that little grocerette at the exit?"

So we pulled in to Hockney's Market, and I chose these glasses because they were the only style offered except for some with blue mirror lenses.

Of course, I didn't get to use them reading much that day, because once we got all set up with the folding chairs unfolded and the plaid blanket spread out and the cooler nestled under the umbrella's shade, and once I had started into the book's introduction, there just seemed to be too many things the author was getting at that I had to tell Libby. And of course she kept coming across important questions to ask me, about points the author made in *Image Formation in the 1800s,* and really very little of either book got read. We finally gave it up and dragged the lunch and the folding canvas chairs down to the water and ate our kippers and rolls and grapes with the water eddying around our ankles and the metal chair rims sinking gradually into the wet sand.

After lunch Libby went off on one of her marathon beach walks, camera slung around her neck, her long stride quickly making her disappear into the misty afternoon beach air. I always reveled in watching her walk, especially across a beach bristling with sandpipers and terns and gulls.

I hated that moment when she'd just vanish into the horizon, which Libby said was called the moment of attenuation; but it was nearly worth it for the moment on the opposite end of the telescope, when she'd be approaching me. If I happened to be sitting on one of those folding chairs and looking around I'd see her, at first tiny and very far away, barely recognizable, except to me. When I looked up again I'd be able to make out a few details, her blue shorts and striped bathing suit top, and then I could see her features, see her waving her hand as if to say, "Don't watch me," the way she must have when she was sixteen and taller and smarter than all the boys. Then, at last, here she was, real and breathing and alive next to me, the sun and the sound of the waves and everything all around us salty and wet.

One time I imagined what it might be like if she never reappeared from that mist, if I just sat there and sat there, walked down to the water, walked back to the blanket, read some of my book, ate an apple, a cookie, and the earth's spin made the big hot sun appear to drift across the white sky, and then the air cooled and she still didn't return. Would I just accept that it had all been a dream, a precisely and deeply detailed dream, and pack up the cooler, umbrella, and books, and drive myself home?

No. I knew I'd wait for her all night, wrap myself in the blanket, watch the stars load up the southern summer sky. I knew I'd lie there until she returned, that I'd wake to find her sleeping beside me, wake weeping in the relief of her arms.

On Memorial Day I put on those sunglasses, and looked in the mirror; I could hardly see my own face. Everything was dark, except for the sliver of light where the lenses met.

I went out wearing them Memorial Day morning. I walked into downtown Durham as if I had never set foot there before, as if I were some stranger who had just arrived on the Greyhound from D.C. I went into Earle's Variety, where I always picked up the morning *Tribune*, and the girl at the counter— Earle's daughter, I'd always thought— looked right through me, just handed me my change without a word.

I walked south on Main Street. Everything was closed, all the shops with their shiny glass windows flat and shut against the holiday. The flags hung limp in the still air.

I walked into the Cameron, where Libby and I would get a booth Sundays, and swung up on a stool. I took off the shades.

Sure enough, I didn't recognize the kid who came over with a menu and asked if I wanted coffee. I said yes, black, and he brought me a cup of dark liquid, and I sipped at it, startled by how hot and bitter it was. I told myself I liked it that way.

I looked at the paper I'd gotten at Earle's. I thought I didn't know anyone's name, or who was the mayor and did I like him or not, and why there was a photo of a woman waving to such a large crowd on page one. I thought I didn't recognize the layout or the type or any of the bylines, and all the stores and insurance companies advertising their business looked unfamiliar. I wondered where my insurance was, or if I had any, or even if I had a car or a house to worry about.

I ate my eggs on cheese grits, which before had always just seemed disgusting, all drippy and yellow and sticky.

The bill was $6.90, and I didn't feel cheated. I left a nice tip, put on my sunglasses, and walked out to the sidewalk, which was probably very bright white in the day's rising heat, but which looked cool and dark and serene to me in my shades.

I threw the paper into a trash can. It never happened, I said under my breath. It was a dream, exquisitely detailed, I said to myself, and you put on your shades and packed up your things and drove yourself home.

HOME

Home again, home again, jiggety-jog. The worst part was pulling up the driveway, turning my face toward the wide front porch as if I'd see Libby there, waiting for me. Or the worst was walking up to the back door, thinking I saw a little scrap of white paper—a note, a note from Libby!—tacked to the wood, then realizing it was just the sunlight through the screen.

Maybe the worst was unlocking the door, stepping into the cool silence. The kitchen, the hallway, then the living room yawning its mouth to me.

The house looked spare since Libby had moved out: just a scattering of furniture, a club chair, a bookcase, a couple of Libby's photos still up on the wall.

The only room that was still the same was my study, and sometimes I'd just sit at my desk, staring at my collection of shells and sea glass. Or I'd look through my books: *The History of Ectoskeletals, The Encyclopaedia of Oceanography, Crest Height and Trough Depth in Atlantic Waves.* Sometimes I'd just sit there and look around at my things, trying to remember that this is who I'd been even before Libby.

But I still had the photo on my desk: Libby in her heavy blue cable sweater, one hand jammed deep in the pocket of her long khaki walking shorts, the other hand wrapped around the rail of the ferry. Her broad shoulders, her height, the whole enigmatic and electric self of her staring out at me, more real than anything else in the room.

On Memorial Day, I came home again, walked through the rooms. Even though I knew Libby wouldn't have come by, I still had that little hope, and when I saw there really was no note, no sign from her—she wasn't sitting on the striped club chair, rattling the ice in her iced tea—again, my mind started racing, like it had when I quit smoking: as if my neuroreceptors were searching for something, something just around the corner. Some relief.

I opened the front door and sat on the porch steps. Every time we spoke, she told me she still felt the passion, the "abiding love," the nearly mystical, inexplicable recognition we'd felt with one another.

So why leave? Why move to an apartment on Berkeley Street, taking her books and her clothes, her tall bicycle, her thick scent of coffee and lemon soap and her jar of sharply pointed pencils and her insatiable questions about the world?

"It's just too painful to try to be close to you when

you're so remote. I can't stand it to keep trying when you're sealed away from me."

That. Again. And: "Of course I think of you constantly—sometimes when I pick up my camera, I see you there through the lens. You're always walking across my vision, walking up to me at the research desk, sitting in front of me at the movie theater, running alongside my bike."

Always? Even in the depth of Doris' tight little mouth?

I rested my head against the porch rail. I wanted a cigarette.

SECRET

I didn't tell anyone that I was still expending a considerable amount of energy driving over to Libby's new apartment, in the hopes of seeing her Land Rover there without any evidence of Doris. Dr. Israel and Pat and Taylor had scolded me for driving by all through January and February, till I finally went out to stay with Joanna in California. After being there for three weeks, I felt better, but as soon as I was back, I was pulled again to Libby's new street.

As I'd approach, first I'd see the building's pitched black roof above the trees. Then, the white clapboards would appear; as I'd near the driveway, my right leg would start shaking, and then, wham. Doris' car like a door in my face. I'd pull into the driveway, then back out onto the street, my leg and my hands shaking so badly that sometimes I'd stall out.

I knew everyone was right; driving by only made things worse, if things could really be worse in a nightmare. Does a nightmare degenerate, and degenerate, till the sleeper wakes?

Libby's new place was near my lab at Duke, or at least not far tom it, kind of on the way. By Memorial Day I'd developed a finely tuned system, and I had certain rules for my own self-protection.

First of all, I didn't talk about it. Back in the winter, I'd get so panicked after seeing Doris' car again, parked behind Libby's, that I'd drive home and call Pat or Taylor and say: I can't breathe. But then they'd ask what had happened, and I'd say: I drove by, and Doris' car was there. They were sick of it; even Pat had managed by then to stop calling Joy Anne, and finally Taylor said: "What do you expect? They're involved with each other." So I stopped talking about it.

My second rule was that I never drove by at night. When I'd first started driving by in January, I'd see Doris' ugly little tan car parked behind Libby's Land Rover, and then see looming into my imagination, so clearly, Doris lying on Libby's back, the new white-and-blue sheets Libby had bought all twisted beneath and around them. And then I'd have to drive home, lie on the couch in the empty silent house, and watch the occasional car lights shine across the living room walls.

Sleep was a difficult enough proposition, without knowing right then, that moment.

My third rule was that I only drove by once a day. Before I made the rules, I'd leave the house early in the morning, around five, having finally given up my meager attempt at sleep, and there was Doris' car. In the afternoon, on my lunch break, Libby's Land Rover would maybe be gone, but Doris' car was still there. Or Libby's would be behind Doris', as if they had swapped places during the night. Infuriated, I'd try to figure it out. Was Doris in there alone? Had they gone out somewhere in Libby's car? Had Doris quit her lousy little proofreading job at the *Triangle Weekly*?

But I just kept wanting the relief of knowing it had stopped. I wanted to wake already from the nightmare, to wake to Libby stretched again around me, to turn to her and say, What a preposterous dream I had. I at least wanted to drive by early some Sunday morning and see only Libby's Land Rover hulking in the driveway, quiet and protective and alone.

Most nights the images of Libby and Doris trailed across my vision, inescapable; I'd try to think of other things, but each thought tripped a switch leading me back. I'd remember how as a girl, I'd lie in bed, unable to sleep, the whir of the fan rustling the warm air around my bedroom; how I'd turn to the white wall, pretending I was in an Eskimo's igloo on the North Pole. Now, grown, I remembered how the igloo is made of bricks, how the light chinks through the edges—how like a tent, a tent that Libby and I woke in, leaf shadows against the green nylon.

On that Friday morning before Memorial Day weekend, I got out of my car in Libby's driveway and looked into the back seat of the Land Rover. Sure enough, there were the neatly folded towels and the striped canvas beach chairs, and a pile of books, all ready to go. The book on top of the pile, *Shells Under Water*, a children's book illustrated with watercolor close-ups of marine life: the pink-orange starfish, the cobalt mussels. I knew every page because I'd given it to Libby.

J O U R N A L

After Memorial Day, I made one more entry in my journal, sitting in the half-bare living room, under the little white Christmas lights Libby had trimmed around the front window, looking at the human spine she'd stolen from the *Tribune*'s research department for my thirtieth birthday.

I could pack
that spine in my suitcase and
zip up the sides, wrap it in my
bathrobe or swaddle it in
t-shirts, shorts, the sort of
clothing I'll be draping on my
body soon. My body's turning
to a bag of bones, pants loosen-
ing around my waist as if

they've grown large all night.
Mornings, I don't dare to stand
before the mirror anymore, for
fear that there'll be nothing
there.

All Libby's photos are
gone—turned facedown or put
away. Now, I don't want a trace.

Does Amnesia really exist?
It sounds like the name of a
beautiful island with dry hot
breezes rustling the palm
leaves. The susurration of
memory's cessation. There's a
10:10 ship that's setting sail for
Amnesia, where memory
plagues no one, where I'll sit
on a wrought-iron chair and
look out, out, and whenever
someone near me calls a
woman's name, I'll say, "Do
you want me?" Amnesia with
its resident Amnesians who
wander house to house, friend
to friend, lover to lover, never
sure which spot is theirs or to
whom it is that they belong,
but comfortable in not knowing, every place and person
equally unknown.

What about that woman
who just disappeared from her
life and turned up in Florida
someplace, found by a state
trooper weeping in her car by
the side of the highway? They
brought her back. What's the
lesson there?

"I was almost to the ferry
to Amnesia," I imagine her
saying quietly in the patrol car.
What's the lesson there? Leave
the car at home; they'll trace
the plates. Assume a name.
Dye your hair. Change your
face.

VANISHING

If I were Libby I wouldn't come back, I thought as I sat on the plaid cotton blanket, the Sunday evening sun stretching long shadows from the sweet bay magnolias and flowering dogwoods across the lawn of Duke Gardens, the closely cropped grass spiking a stiff ledge underneath me. The June air was cooling. I buttoned my sweater.

I was waiting for Libby to return from the latrines on the other side of the arbor, to come back to our sad little picnic. I was waiting, and wishing that the last time I saw her—lifting herself from the blanket with that ineffable awkward grace she has, brushing her blond curls back from her forehead—would be *the* last time I saw her. The really last time. We could save ourselves the rest of this terrible farewell, which had started the day before.

Maybe it had truly started months before, back in De-

cember, or perhaps the trouble had been gestating years before that; maybe we'd just been doomed from the start.

Like everything else between us, even this farewell talk
wasn't simple, having started on Saturday and reconvened
Sunday. And still I wasn't even sure as I lay back, propped
up on my elbows, that this would be the absolute last time
that I'd see Libby. I couldn't imagine there ever being a last
time for the two of us, after our finding each other and feeling that wash of familiarity mingled with a thrill of dis-
covery, then spending five years piecing together our life.
Libby said she couldn't imagine it either, still.

But I knew that the past six months had changed something in me. Knowing she was with Doris—or at least, in
Libby's words, that they were "exploring things with each
other"—made me crazy enough, like having the wind
knocked out of me, over and over. But worse were the times
when I'd break down and call Libby, only to hear her continue her declarations of love and devotion to me. It didn't
make sense, and I couldn't push it all into place so that it
would make sense. Our conversations always ended up the
same, with me saying, "But then why are you with Doris?"
The confusion that infused me was too familiar, and I could
feel something in me metallicizing to a steel wire that lay
lodged in my chest.

Somehow I knew this picnic supper wouldn't turn anything around for either of us.

Face it, I'd told myself sternly that morning, nothing
you do or say is going to change her. You can't change her.
You can't change her. It had become my mantra months

ago, and I'd chant it to myself on my way to the lab in the morning, or hum it into a song as I drove by her apartment, or somehow resisted driving by. My right leg had taken to trembling now whenever I drove, a trembling that started in the bone of my kneecap and shook and shimmied till my whole leg was going.

Like everything else, driving hadn't been easy lately.

But I'd gotten through, gotten over to this point, the point where I was pretty firm with myself sometimes, chanting that mantra or the other one: forget, forget, forget. Sometimes I thought about how Pat had survived after Joy Anne left her, the Saturday night when she called to say she just could not stand knowing that Joy Anne was with a man at that moment. I'd dwell on how Pat had made it through intact. Alive. Breathing. Waking in the morning and showing up for work. And more than that: I'd think about how much integrity Pat and I both had, neither one of us really doing anything all that self-destructive, neither one of us turning to some new lover, or to cigarettes or bourbon.

But the self-congratulatory properties of a ride on the moral high road only go so far, and I fell back into my vain hope when I finally saw Libby on Saturday at her new apartment. I'd made the appointment with her ostensibly so I could tell her I'd decided to move to Chapel Hill.

"I've decided I shouldn't keep living in Durham. It's too terrible, opening the *Trib* and seeing your photos, worrying if I'll run into you and Doris, seeing a poster for a piano concerto and knowing you'll go with her. I just can't stand it," I'd said, sitting in her familiar mission chair, looking at her on her new sofa. It was beige, and I couldn't help but wonder if Doris had offered her opinion about the color choice. Or the softness.

I kept looking about the room, looking for evidence of Doris, but other than the new sofa, everything looked just like Libby: clean, and in a way, spare, even with her favored objects scattered around—her old daguerreotypes of seaside scenes on the wall, her painted ceramic bowls propped up between the books on the built-in shelves, the stained-glass mobile her aunt had made when Libby was born hanging over the window seat, and all her papers and contact sheets and plastic canisters of film strewn across her Shaker table. She even had the collage I'd made of sea things in the window, and the photo of us on the ferry to Okracoke stood on the bookshelf.

And Libby looked me in the eye in a way I'd only seen a couple of times before, and those eyes, those blue eyes that pick up all the light around her and fracture it into chips of heat, were sadder than I'd seen them, and the strong bones of her face seemed to melt into the face of a child. I was startled by this, startled by her crying, and surprised to feel my own face open to her in a new way. Surprised by how much there was to say, by how thick the feeling still was between us. I felt my heart, my heart that was so weary with the weight of Libby's absence and of Doris' presence, lifting, dropping, lifting in my chest.

I guess you could say I got my hopes up.

All of which goes to explain why I'd stood in the check-out line at the Winn-Dixie Sunday at noon, preparing for this second part of our talk, this picnic that could very well mark the beginning of our new life together. I'd forgotten all my mantras, and I was hoping. Unbridled by caution or fear or sensibility, my hope came pelting out of the stable and started around the track at a full gallop, then broke right through the fence and sped across the racetrack park ing lot, across the adjacent fields, and into the hazy distance.

With me hanging on for dear life to a thin and slippery mane.

Now, lying propped up on my elbows on the plaid blanket, the Sunday evening slipping closer across Duke Gardens, I knew that this had really been the farewell picnic, not the picnic of reunion and reconciliation. Libby had said she still couldn't come back, was still too afraid of how deeply I could edge into myself. So I lay on the spread and looked at the prospect of waking to another Monday in the house without Libby shaking her curly head in my face, saying, "If I let you, you'd sleep more hours than one day has, girl," without our breakfast chatter, the rye toast and light coffee, without her kiss as we bolted out the kitchen door. And the week loomed into a vast gulf before me, the days and weeks after that all coiled and hissing at the gulf's bottom.

Now the mosquitos were biting at the border of bare ankle between my jeans and my plaid sneakers, and I wished I'd kept my mantra going. I wished Libby would just use the latrine and keep on walking, out of the gardens and back to her apartment, to call Doris and go back to living in her vortex of confusion.

I wished then that the amnesia that had apparently washed over her, allowing her to wake beside Doris, would suddenly flood her, and she wouldn't even recognize me or our spread or the beach chairs when she came back, but would just walk past.

Maybe it wasn't so much that I wished Libby would just walk away. Maybe I wished that *I* could be the one to disappear.

So that's what I did. I stood up, looked around. Libby was nowhere in sight—maybe she *had* just walked off, I thought for a brief panicky moment. Dusk was now spreading over the gardens; I hadn't realized until I stood up how little light was left. The sky was that deep Sunday blue going black, just on the cusp of color seeping into empty space.

I walked in the opposite direction of the way Libby had gone, toward the neatly clipped boxwood around the pond where the fat goldfish swam. There were a couple of stone benches on the other side of the hedgerow where I could sit and keep a view of our things, yet still be hidden from Libby's sight. Like most mammals, I knew where the good hiding places were.

I crouched behind the hedgerow; I was glad I'd put on my dark blue sweater and was wearing my black jeans. I could stay there, concealed. I wanted to see how long Libby would wait for me, and what, if anything, she'd call out into the darkness, her voice rising with fear and confusion when she realized I was gone.

But I didn't wait. I suddenly didn't want to know any more. I stood, turned, and slipped between the boxwood hedges, then stepped quietly through the towering rhododendrons and ran.

MOTEL

At first I couldn't even think, and I briefly wondered if I should be driving in such a blurred condition, but what else could I do? Go home and sit on the couch again, knowing that Libby had probably left the park, driven back to her apartment, and called Doris? Go home and call Pat and then Joanna out in California, and try to explain again that feeling of having all the air forced from my lungs? Go home and somehow manage to stave it off, make my bed again on the sofa, wake on Monday and drive by Libby's looking for Doris' car, looking to see if the shades were still drawn?

No. After I left the gardens I went back to the house, and got some old cardboard boxes down from the attic, trying not to look at our camping gear or the Christmas decorations or the boxes of photos Libby had left. Then I went through the house, tossing in everything Libby had given me or that had been part of our lives together—the ceramic mug with the roses twined along the handle, the black-and-white photos she'd taken in China and Italy, the few books she'd neglected to take with her: *The History of Photojournalism*, *Light Refraction and Speed*, and even her recent acquisition, *Just the Facts*, which she'd gotten when she picked up some shifts at the research department for the *Durham Morning Tribune*. I let our history fall into the boxes in a jumbled pile, not wrapping anything, just letting it collect. I wanted the rooms empty of anything I'd thought we had.

When I was done, I looked around. The house actually looked pretty nice like this, I thought; it looked clean and welcoming and well organized.

I packed a couple of bags of clothes, leaving behind the things that had been favorites of Libby's: my flowered summer shirts and plaid sneakers, my white turtleneck sweater, even my red baseball jacket with the madras lining. At the last minute, I'm not sure why, I threw in the old blue sweater of hers I still had. It still smelled like her.

And then I shut the door behind me.

Of course, Doris' car was sitting in its spot behind Libby's when I drove by for the last time. I tanked up with gas, and soon I was headed west on Route 40. The night was very bright with the nearly full moon, and I could see the fields running out north and south around me, then folding up into hills, the shadowy moonlight filling pockets between the hillocks, the occasional brick farmhouse suddenly appearing before me, kudzu-covered.

The landscape drifted into dark as I headed west, into the mountains.

I came to Asheville near dawn. I'd only been here once before, the summer before I started grad school at Duke. Before I met Libby.

I pulled in to the Days Inn and brought in one of my bags. When the man pushed the registration card and a pen across the counter to me, I panicked for a minute, wondering what the hell I was doing. Then I thought of that woman who disappeared last year and turned up later in Florida, and something from my memorization of binomial nomenclature rose up in my head.

"Virginia Didelphis," I signed boldly. I made up some numbers and letters for the license plate of my car, smiling a little when I remembered the motto on the plate: "First in Flight."

"You have a good rest, Miss Didelphis," the man said.

"I'm sure I will," I lied, then rode the elevator up and unlocked my door.

I liked how sterile my room was, cleansed of all the emotions that had ever been felt there, all the fights and lovemaking and plain rest of weary travelers wiped clean, leaving no mark on the perfectly made bed.

I'd never been comfortable in motel rooms. One of Libby's complaints about me toward the end was that we'd hardly ever made love in a motel on any of our trips. "They just make my skin crawl—I don't know why," I'd said as we pulled into the driveway after a weekend away.

"I don't understand this," Libby said, shutting off the engine of the Land Rover. "I mean, what else am I supposed to think, other than that you just don't want to be with me?"

"Don't be ridiculous. You know I want to be with you away or at home or anywhere." I could feel myself sinking lower in the seat, the panic rising in my chest. Why *did* I have this aversion to motels, and travel? I shut my eyes and tried to figure it out. I really didn't know then that as with so many things, this fear was an eruption from my childhood, that it could be neatly traced to the nights my mother would pile me and Joanna in the car to drive through motel parking lots looking for Dad's old MG. My imagination reeled out the rest from there. But I didn't put the whole thing together until the end of that last year with Libby: not the motel rooms, or my dodge whenever Libby would ask about Dad, or that cold weight in my stomach I felt sometimes when Libby would lean in to kiss me.

Now, I liked the uniform sterility of the room. It could absorb anything. It was blank and boring and had nothing in it to remind me.

I took off all my clothes and got in the shower and turned on the water, hot. I let the water fill my hair, weigh my head down. I felt my jaw clamp up and my eyes fill, and I hugged my arms to my chest. The crying was just something physical happening to me, and eventually it stopped. I turned the water off, stepped out, wrapped myself in the big white motel towel, and fell onto the bed and into a deep, nearly comatose sleep.

PHONE CALL

The first thought to jump to my brain when I jolted awake was the familiar blade: Libby's gone. For that moment on the verge from sleep to waking, I thought I was on the couch in Durham where I'd slept since January, and I turned, expecting to push my face against the soft blue-and-white-striped sofa cushions, expecting to see the room yellow in the early light, to hear the thud of the *Tribune* hitting the porch. Everything I'd grown used to: my little comforts.

Instead, I raised myself onto my elbows on the wide, crisp bed. A sheet of light stained the room through the stiff gold curtains.

I hadn't exactly been planning this. My planning abilities, such as they'd been, were pretty much shot to hell along with everything else in January. Planning to squeeze the toothpaste from the tube and onto the brush while I stared down into the sink was an effort at first, say till April. Sure, it did get better, and I kept reminding myself of that. I kept showing up for work, and by March I was able to actually talk to the students working in the marine lab or catalog the most recent acquisition of ectoskeletals. Pat and I even planned to go to a movie a week ahead, and we both got to the theater on time, on the right night.

But planning to vanish would have taken far more wherewithal than I possessed at that point. And sometimes things work out better when they're spontaneous: think of all the research trips I'd carefully executed underwater, prepared to uncover data on the senses of crabs, and then that one serendipitous swim that proved a breakthrough in the muscle structure of pelagic fish. Or worse: compare the great romance of Libby and me—all that longing for the first couple of years, that yearning for the day it would all fall into place, perfect, precise, irrevocable—to her happening to share a ride with Doris to that damn newspaper conference, staying in the hotel bed for the weekend, and then maintaining whatever the hell it is they've achieved all this time. The best-laid schemes o' mice and men . . .

I could look up the whole quote and see if it really backs up my point here or not, if I had my books with me, because if I had my books I'd have my Steinbeck, and if I had my Steinbeck I could just look on the title page and maybe the quote would be there. Sometimes I hate all the reference and research techniques I have stuffed in my head.

Or I could call Libby at the research desk at the *Tribune* and ask her to look in *Bartlett's*.

That thought made me laugh, and I knew it would have made her laugh too, and that made me miss her again. I could imagine calling her, hearing her businesslike answer: "Research."

"Hi Libby, it's me," I'd say, just like I used to, just like Doris probably did now, and she'd catch herself as she starts to say "Hi you," or "Hey!" in her big bold way. She'd be surprised, because by now she knows I've vanished, and everyone's looking for me and wondering if I'll float up from the depths of the Neuse River this summer or what.

She'd stammer out my old name in surprise, that hint of a lisp simmering on her "s."

"Listen, I don't want to keep you," I'd say, pleased at my double entendre and wondering if she caught it. "I'm actually calling you in your official capacity." And I'd ask about the quote. "You see, I don't have my books, because I just vanished, and I really couldn't take much with me."

But she'd know that. She was, after all, the last person to see me. And by then the line would be dead, anyway, and I'd just be sitting there listening to that hollow dead-line sound with the wind that blows through my empty chest now blowing through the telephone wire, too, threatening to take over the whole world, and I'd be looking at my fingers holding the buttons pressed deep into the cradle of the motel phone.

SELLING THE CAR

I didn't have much to clean out of my Toyota. In the motel parking lot I went through everything. I left the red emergency light in the trunk, I lifted the plaid picnic blanket to my face, breathed in deeply once, then folded it and put it on the felt mat on the trunk floor.

Inside the car, I opened the glove compartment. I separated everything into three piles: maps and car warranties to leave there; little things to take with me, like the tin of mint candies and an old postcard from Joanna; and things of Libby's—a painted Italian tile, her horn-rimmed shades, and the little notes she'd written to me in her angular lettering. I jammed these into a plastic bag I'd found on the car floor, tied the bag up, and tucked it under the passenger seat.

I pulled out of the parking lot, followed the road along,

and sure enough, I came to the Asheville strip. I knew I would: every modern town has one, and Asheville's was no different from Durham's or Charlotte's, with its Krispy Kreme and Grits to Go and gas stations and car lots, all lined up in a row of tremendous ugliness, a sprawling testament to humanity's miraculous ability to create and then withstand, even encourage, the least aesthetically pleasing environment possible.

"When I'm with you I can even stand driving on the strip," I'd told Libby that first summer we were together, glancing at her knees resting bent against my dashboard as I drove us to the Denny's all-you-can-eat breakfast.

Now, I looked out the windshield, and imagined the countryside as it once was: open meadows with flocks of passenger pigeons filling the sky like clouds.

I sliced across the lanes, and pulled into a Toyota dealer's lot, shut off the car for the last time, and walked toward the big-windowed showroom.

As soon as I saw the old Bel Air hunkered down in the lot, I knew it was just what I needed. I could tell it had once gleamed a shiny red, one of those 1950s colors with a name like Candy Apple. The driver's door was unlocked, and the handle clicked appealingly when I pushed it in; I was surprised at how heavy the door was, at the weight of it. I slid in behind the big round steering wheel, breathing deeply the musty old-car smell that rose from the white leather seats. It smelled like the first car I remember, Mom's old Buick, and for a moment I could almost smell her Chanel No. 5 mingling with her vodka.

The key was in the ignition, and I turned it, and the engine started up big and powerful, like something that could take care of me.

The Chevy's door slammed solidly shut behind me when I got out. As I walked into the showroom a skinny, solicitous man came toward me, brushing crumbs from his tie and white shirt.

"It'll be a hot one today," he said, now wiping his pinched brow with a white handkerchief. I was already feeling my skin contract from the cold of the air they had blasting around. I wondered if the special showroom cars needed extra cold for some reason, or if it was some kind of sales technique to keep the room cold but have the salesman pretend it was hot. Some kind of toying with the parameters of reality.

Then again, I knew my ability to determine who was telling the truth and who was lying could certainly bear some scrutiny.

"You like to keep it warm in here, do you?" I asked, pleased to see the salesman's eyebrows lift in a single line of surprise. Maybe I'd fare better if I went along with the world's propensity for duplicity.

I told the salesman I wanted to check the Blue Book value of my car. He snapped a wallet-size version from his breast pocket, licked his finger, and found the page. One of the first times I saw Libby, she'd licked her finger like that, to find the page in a photography book at the Duke library. The blue book said "$8,124" next to my car's model and year. More than I'd thought.

"That's all?" I said.

"Well, more with your optionals, your air, your FM

stereo cassette, cellular phone, automatic cup holders," he said. "But we should really talk first about what you'd like to trade it in for. Now, this year we've got some super models—"

I cut him off.

"Actually, I really can't trade it for something new. You know, it's my sister's car. She gave it to me a couple of months ago, when she knew she was going to pass . . . Well, now that she's passed away this week I—" I paused for effect, drew in a deep breath to regain my strength after uttering the unbearable words. "And we can't get into the estate right away, so we decided to sell the car to settle up a few matters." I thought the plural first person added an air of authority: I'm not just some nut traveling alone; I've got a bunch of bereaved people waiting back at the house.

"Oh, I see. Terribly, terribly sorry. Such a tragedy. So young."

"Yes," I said, drawing in another deep breath. "Now, the car has air, FM stereo, power windows. I was thinking if you give me a good deal, maybe I'd trade it for that old Chevy out front. Are you interested?"

"Well, you see, we have to check it all out, have our mechanics go over every little thing, and then there's the paperwork. Plus, that Chevy's in mint condition . . ."

My chest started closing in. There it was, that pitch forward. I was trapped. I couldn't wait for all that procedure but I sure as hell couldn't keep driving this car, the car in which Libby and I had fought, made love, eaten chicken to go and drunk iced tea, the car permeated now with the scent of her, the sound of her. The car in which we'd lunged late onto the last ferry to Okracoke how many times? How many?

I realized I was just staring at the salesman's tie.

"I'm sorry," I said truthfully. "It's been such a difficult time, and I'm so tired."

The salesman handed me his handkerchief. I blew my nose as loudly as I could.

"Listen, will you just give me four thousand and that Chevy, and we'll call it even? Would you do that for me?"

With the cash in my pocket I walked into the Asheville branch of North Carolina Trust, and closed out our accounts. I wondered what Libby would think when she deposited her check the next week. I imagined her at first irate at the presumed mistake, the error of the computer. Maybe she'd remember how I'd always warned her that computers would be the demise of everything good on the planet. I imagined her stunned as she realized what I'd done, but then, I thought, why hasn't she done this already? Why has she kept me threaded to her with subtotaling and totaling of numbers, addition and subtraction ticking us together even now?

The money from our accounts seemed a little tainted, contaminated by Libby, by my memory of her. I put some of the cash in one suitcase, some in the other, got into the Chevy, and headed north on Route 23.

NEW CAR

I was scared, at first, that the old Chevy would break down, and I'd be stranded on some highway in some state with a 1950 Chevy and no old-timey service stations to go with it. Just those damn self-serves where the gal behind the glass window knows even less than I do about auto repair and at best knows how to get to the nearest Jiffy Lube.

But I was glad I'd bought it. I figured, why not? Why not get something that was built before Libby was born? And why not buy a big swaggering car that could be more like a companion to me than just a method of transportation?

Besides, I didn't have anything to fear anymore. Maybe all postsuicidals feel that way. It's really great—it gives you a real sense of, not bravery exactly, and not recklessness, quite, but something in between the two. If I'd survived my own best attempts at dying, it probably just wasn't in the cards for me to perish young.

The car smelled wonderful, musty and dusty, and I liked the smooth, worn white leather seats with red piping. The steering wheel once had been shiny silver. The whole car was huge, and reminded me for a minute of how I'd felt with Libby, when we'd be walking and she'd tower over me, or how she'd shelter us both with her big red umbrella, or how she'd lift me in her arms and carry me from the kitchen to the couch.

I blinked, and turned on the radio, expecting songs from 1950 to come out. But instead it was Mozart.

JOURNAL

I'd left my journal behind, packed in one of the cardboard cartons I'd taped shut and stacked in the attic. But even as I moved forward, catapulting toward Amnesia, I couldn't quite snap the habit of making notes. I didn't want to keep these messages: I'd find myself writing on a paper napkin or a matchbook, some scrap of trash, which I'd let fall and flutter away from my hand, into the world of lost things, that mysterious realm where so much of what I'd loved had accumulated. I liked thinking of the trail I left behind, the meal receipts and newspaper margins cluttered by my words.

ANOTHER DAY

There was
nothing to it, nothing else for
me to do.
   One week you're there, an-
swering the phone, opening
the mail, tending to the plants
or to what your neighbors or
your friends expect. You're
waking earlier each morning
to that repeating nightmare.
Your friends tire of always
reaching in, and each time you
beg off anyway.
   Look at my face. I've
walked out of my life.

L I B R A R Y

I walked into the library as if I'd never set foot in one before. It was in a small town on the edge of West Virginia. It
was a little library, but the town boasted a college and a hos-
pital, so I thought the library might have a *Wescott and
Williamson's General Medica.*

Besides, I was tired of driving aimlessly east, then tacking north, then west again. I had no plans. I could stop at a
library, at a grocery store, at the town hall and register to
vote if I felt like it. But this stop had a purpose.

I pulled open the heavy glass door, and walked into the
cavernous room. On one wall stood an old oak card catalog,
and across the room there was a desk with a little black sign
with white letters spelling out "Reference."

I thought for a minute that Libby would be sitting there
behind the desk. She's been following me, and then she

headed me off, knowing I'd be here, I thought for a minute. She'll stand up, open her arms to me, and I'll just fall in. But it wasn't her, of course. It was a balding man with glasses.

"Do you have *Wescott and Williamson's General Medica?*" I asked. My voice felt scratchy from disuse.

He looked surprised, as if not many people wandered in asking for obscure medical texts. "As a matter of fact, we do," he said, and I went traipsing after him. He handed me the heavy blue book, then disappeared, the way librarians are supposed to.

I looked in the index. "Amnesia." I turned to page 1030. It was in the chapter on acute confusional states, and that seemed about right.

I read through the pathophysiology: "Most cases result from insult to the Central Nervous System, and cause partial or complete memory loss without impairment of other functions . . ." That's what I wanted—to fill myself with entirely new memories that would be utterly unrelated to Libby Grant and her gravitational pull on me.

Just as I was beginning to think I'd have to do some real damage to achieve this, that I'd have to really let go of the wheel of the Chevy as I rounded a curve, I saw the paragraph on transient global amnesia.

"Often of unknown etiology, transient global amnesia sometimes results from emotional trauma, travel in a motor vehicle, immersion in hot or cold water, or increased cerebrovascular flow. Patient is frequently bewildered, and persists in asking questions about past events. On formal examination, patient indicates intact immediate recall but severely impaired long-term memory."

It went on to say attacks only last at most twelve hours, but still, it gave me some hope. Maybe I could work at it backward. Maybe forcing myself to not remember, combined with travel in a motor vehicle and immersion in hot or cold water, could institute amnesia in me. And maybe it wouldn't have to be transient.

I looked around the library. It was pretty quiet; not many people were coming out on a hot day to read up. I wondered for a moment if this was Friday—no, it was Saturday. Saturday, and I could see Libby and Doris driving to the beach, the back seat piled with towels and Libby's red cooler and all their books.

I tore the thin page from the book, folded it, and slipped it into the back pocket of my shorts. My god. Libby would have been horrified, then thrilled because it was sudden, sudden and shocking to see me do such a reckless thing.

No. Get in the car. Drive fast. Find a cold, quick-currented river. Dive in. Freeze or boil it out.

It never happened, I told myself as I pressed the gas pedal hard to the floor. You were born January 1, or February 29, in Albuquerque, New Mexico, or La Junta, Colorado, or way up north in Michigan. Maybe you studied English literature in college, or got an advanced degree in economics. You read in the paper about a woman from Durham who disappeared. It wasn't you. It wasn't you.

M A P

It was near two a.m. when I stopped in Pennsylvania for
gas. While I stood in the cramped store, in the wheeze of
diesel and sigh of trucks' brakes, waiting for the man ahead
of me to sign his credit slip, I saw the rack of maps. "USA
and CANADA," one spelled out in red letters on a blue
field.

I plucked it out. "This too, please," I said in a phony
French accent, and paid.

When I got back to the car, I didn't want to look at the
map right away. For one thing, I knew my eyes would be
drawn to that lower right-hand corner, damn, as if I could,
by peering at the dry sheet of printed paper, see Libby bi-
cycling to the newspaper building, tiny wheels spinning
across the page. But I also wanted to savor the map, ritualize the unfolding paper, the way I'd savored the postcards

Libby had sent me at the lab in Beaufort. I'd pick up my mail, but wouldn't let myself look at her writing, or really at the front of the card, there with Dave and everyone chattering around me. I'd wait till I was alone on the beach or back in my own room, then read her words, or the words she chose to quote: "Exposed on the cliffs of the heart," she had written on the back of a card with a photo she'd made of a scattering of sea rubble, twisting seaweed knotted around wind-driven shells and rock.

No. Maybe if I could ritualize looking at the map I could find someplace to go toward; maybe I could torque some control over all this motion.

I drove awhile longer, the dark countryside rising and flattening around me. Finally I saw a sign: "Scenic Lookout," and I pulled off the road. I left the car running, got out, and spread the map out across the hood. I wanted the Chevy to be part of this decision.

At first, of course, I did look homeward, to that familiar oblong of North Carolina. But then I remembered again the postcards, and how now Libby's handwriting was becoming familiar to Doris.

On the map, the island seemed almost luminous, as if limned in shimmering silver ink. It wasn't very big—just a tiny fleck of white floating in the center of an egg-shaped lake, so far north I couldn't say if it was in the United States or Canada, the lake itself rivering into the Atlantic. I could see my way there, the webbing routes and highways.

I got back in the car, and pulled back onto the highway. On the radio, a new station crackled into the car, a twanging guitar and fiddle and a man who sounded both energetic and very sad.

After that, my driving had purpose. On the crisp sheet of paper the island floated in the field of blue, a white patch scratched out, hemmed in by numbers signifying water depth and miles.

Early in the mornings as I headed north, just before dawn lit up the sky, I'd pull into a motel or campground. When I lay down in the strange clean bed or in the cocoon of my new sleeping bag, I'd bring the map in with me, unfold it, and stare at the island, imagining it. I'd press the map against my chest, or bury my face in its creases, and when the images of Libby would come flooding in, I'd see the island—green, isolated, cold—waiting for me in its pool of deep blue water, and then I'd sleep.

J O U R N A L

Maybe we're
all pulling toward Amnesia.
Every moment another mem-
ory lofts up, to be later tucked
occipital or frontal, or perhaps
allowed to drift out into the
air a memory balloon lifting
past the tallest houses' black
slate rooftops, up into the
clouds and past the stratos-
phere.

What's the purpose in
our waking every day, unless
it's this gravitation toward

amnesia? Why not say enough
views newly shifted, enough
new memories collecting like a
stack of photos in our heads?

HIGHWAY

And while I drove, Where's Libby? I kept thinking. Where? as I kept pulling west, just because that was the direction I'd started in, the Chevy now rolling me through the Smokies and into Tennessee.

On the night highways, the images that had become so familiar to me in Durham still ran across my vision: Is she now laying her head against her hand the way she liked to when she couldn't sleep? Or is she waking from a dream, turning over, the covers spilling from her shoulders and her breasts? Does she wake every night now to Doris' pale back, and does she ever, in that moment of sleepy bewilderment, think of me? Does she wish that woman next to her was me, me turning to her in her night embrace?

Sometimes I drove right through the night.

And sometimes while I drove I wondered if Dad had

traveled these roads when he'd disappear. Semester break, holiday weekend, or random summer days, he'd simply not show up. Sometimes Mom guessed where he was, or sought my help and Joanna's to ferret out the information. But like the comets he lectured on to high school seniors, he seemed to hit the orbit of our family only on the rare occasion before drifting out again.

I could picture my father rumbling along in the old green MG, the dry dirt spitting out behind him, his other, secret wife in a kerchief in the passenger seat, laughing. He probably took a route like this that summer he went up to Boston to take courses for his Ph.D. Then again, the degree never materialized. Was he lying then, or did he take the courses but only get that far? I still wasn't sure, and now, driving, I felt that old confusion at the missing piece. Of course in a child's way I'd always had my suspicions: other children's fathers stayed around. But it wasn't until last fall, when Libby started threatening to leave, that I started calling Joanna and asking what *she* thought had really happened in our childhood, who our Dad had really been.

"He did the best he could," she started, and I said, "No. He could have done better."

She had told me then about his other wife, how he hadn't simply divorced Mom and remarried, but instead had constructed his secret life around this new woman. Joanna remembered more about our childhood than I could hope to, almost as if she'd had the job of collecting all the bits of information, collating them, protecting them.

Now, I thought about Dad driving these roads or roads like them, driving in his desperate search for something elusive, something better than what he had. The roads he drove would have been quieter, without the glare of the fluorescent lights, without the fast-food joints littering the fields and woods. Near Nashville I turned north, then east, no destination in mind, randomly following the highway signs: Cave City, Corinth, Paintsville.

Sometimes I drive across the night, and on the other side, the darkness seems to lift; then a pale strip of horizon will appear, and the other cars' headlamps gradually become unnecessary, then invisible, and then switch off. Exhausted with my driving and my memory, I pull off the highway, and like some nocturnal beast, I sleep.

BUNNY RIDE

I drove crepuscular, leaving a motel room's cool impersonal cave early in the morning or late in the afternoon, without regard to regular people's schedules. I drove across the late afternoons, dry dust filtering in through the Chevy's air vents, covering the white upholstery, the dash, and me.

While I drove north into the evenings, I remembered dusk drives with Mom and Joanna when we'd visit Maw Maw at her summer place on the Chesapeake Bay, Dad having begged off with some confabulated excuse or another. At the time, I believed he was working hard on the astronomy classes he taught at the high school. I believed he had a lot of papers and tests to prepare.

Once we were at Maw Maw's, everything unruly seemed to drift away: Dad and his constant schemes of getting money or a better house or a new sports car; his erratic schedule; Mom's questioning of us. Even the pains in her legs and stomach seemed to improve at Maw Maw's house.

The best part about those visits was when Mom and Maw Maw would squeeze me and Joanna, bathed and paja-maed, into the front seat with them, and drive the dirt roads looking for bunnies, which we'd see in great abundance by the roadside, their eyes bright in the headlights, startled. Once or twice we even saw a small red fox scuttling into the meadow by the road, and then sometimes, just as the fire-flies began to flicker and Maw Maw first turned the head-lights on, we'd see a deer.

Now I know that a major purpose of these trips was to lull me to sleep. Even then, at six or seven or eight, I didn't travel well, and my restlessness would keep me sitting up in bed, light out but eyes open, listening to the splash of the bay. Sometimes at night I'd just wander around Maw Maw's summer place, looking at how neat everything was, all polished wood and clean white wicker. I'd stand in the screened-in porch sometimes and look out over her yard, at the peony bushes and the blue hydrangeas weighted with the salty night air.

I doubted that I'd ever told anyone these stories, and while I drove I wondered if this was what Libby meant when she said she felt she would never really know me.

Maybe I should have told her about the bunny rides, how I'd drift off to sleep so easily, knowing those rabbits and fox and deer were nearby.

When the headlights of the other cars would pierce too sharply into my eyes, I'd pull over into another anonymous motel, rent a room, and sleep.

J O U R N A L

I could turn
left, then right, then left again,
and I'd be lost, traveling down
some dirt-packed back road on
my way to Reno.

Maybe that's where
Amnesia lies: south, with the
tourniquet of a language I
don't know twisted on its arm,
the arm of an isthmus stretching out into blue gulf waters,
prickly with stingrays and
bloated jellyfish.

Maybe Amnesia isn't such
a pretty picture after all;

maybe it's where swollen
bodies float offshore. Maybe
there's just desert, a brothel,
and a gambling room. Forget
your love, your debts. Here's a
fresh deck. Come on up, and
make your bets.

CAMPING

When I was near the Virginia coast, I stopped at the Wild
Pony Camp Supply House. I bought a cotton sleeping bag
and some waterproof matches, a coffeepot and some uten-
sils. I passed on the little packages of things, the miniature
sewing kit and the tiny salt and pepper envelopes that
Libby had always loved. I wanted everything plain and
unlovable: just an aluminum pot and pan, a simple brown
sleeping bag.

I yawned open the trunk of the Chevy. Inside, there
was enough space for an entire luxury hotel room; my meager supplies looked lost all alone in there.

I got behind the wheel again, and started out of town,
toward Assateague, where Libby had always said ponies ran
wild, still, like the ponies that once roamed the plains out
west, or the sea grass of Okracoke.

By evening I was at the meadows that lead down to the beach. I was starting to enjoy this: me, the old Chevy, and Mozart or some old jazz on the radio. The stations faded in, and out, and back in again, and I didn't bother turning the dial; I just took whatever was offered, even when it was static.

The ponies, it turns out, are only partly wild: they're at a National Seashore, wire fencing around their six hundred acres protecting them from escaping over to the humans' side. The people who had come to visit walked on carefully constructed boardwalks, then peered through binoculars at the animals, who seemed unaware that they were being watched. This made them look a little dumb, and the whole setup was like a living diorama, and I thought, This is what it will all come to: a few parks where we say the animals are wild, redwood boardwalks crossing the meadowlands, a protected habitat with nothing out of place, nothing dangerous. And what choice do we have, now?

When I realized that soon the beach would be flush with sunset, I got in the Chevy and drove farther north along the island, down a dirt road with no sign; then I turned right. This led to another dirt road, where I pushed open a long metal gate and kept on going. Then I pulled over. Here, there were no signs, or mailboxes, or any evidence of humanity's imprint except for the roads themselves. I popped the trunk with my key, took out my new supplies, slammed the trunk, locked the doors, and walked out onto the beach.

I must have walked for a long time through the

scratchy dune grass, watching the herring gulls dip and dive, the smell of the ocean hot and familiar. When I stopped, and turned to see if I could still see the car, it was just a little red splotch resting along the horizon. And then I missed Libby, and felt my chest collapsing in on my lungs, and in that moment I forgot, I forgot why I was here, why I'd had to leave: My god, I thought, why the hell did I leave her? And then I remembered, and I stopped walking, dropped my gear and allowed myself to fall onto my back in the soft sand.

I lay on the sand for a long time, watching the sky go awash with rose, then lavender. I stood, and made a little fire: it started right up. I rolled out my sleeping bag, and sat down on it. I pulled my hair out of the elastic band, and shook it out like a blanket around my shoulders.

Above me, the sky stretched out dark, dark blue, then went black all at once, with stars appearing suddenly. Boom, and it was night, and I was sitting on a sleeping bag next to the ocean, with no protection from the animals. I shut my eyes and remembered crouching over a group of crabs, fifty feet underwater, my tank bubbling behind my head.

I lay down on my back, and immediately remembered Libby above me, and then I pictured myself as I was right in that moment: a small body spread out on a rectangle of cloth beside a beach fire; I imagined the ponies bedding down in the meadow behind me, the unsleeping ocean continuing its heft and plunge in front of me, and then I saw myself and my fire as if from a bird, a huge owl above me, and I saw the red Chevy and the roads that led me here, and everything around me not as it is but as it was, ponies wandering, stamping into the forest, eluding wolves or coyotes. I saw the hills around me spreading into mountain ranges, the Atlantic's blue reach, and then, as if the owl were rising, rising high as the moon, I saw the whole coast of North Carolina and Virginia and Maryland, the Outer Banks a green seam in the blue Atlantic, and the owl was rushing away so fast that soon I could just see the continent of North America, and then the earth, a blue and green orb spinning in the midst of deep black space, and somehow I could still see myself there, on the beach, by my fire and my car, spinning alone on the planet, desperate and solitary.

I woke to the sound of ponies stamping in the meadow, their hooves heavy in the dune grass. A high whinny. The sky was just beginning to fade from black to gray to white. Far off on the horizon, I could see the meadow sand kicked up by the ponies' gallop. And then I saw, closer to me but moving away, the soft white of a snowy owl, lost, knocked off course but heading north, moving, moving against the coming dawn.

P O S S U M

The animal ran straight into my lane. I swerved, but it was
too late; by the time I pulled hard on the big steering wheel,
I'd already felt and heard the thud of my tires against the
body.

I pulled over into the breakdown lane. Luckily there
weren't many cars on the road: it was a secondary highway,
soft-shouldered and pastoral. I'd been driving for hours
since dusk, so I knew it must be pretty late. I shifted into re-
verse and backed up, watching the animal's body come into
view, washed red by the car's pointy taillights.

When I was almost upon it, I stopped and got out.

It was possum, sure enough. I hadn't thought they'd
made it this far north in their radiation from Mexico, but
there was that unmistakable scaly tail curving around its

body, that pointed nose and grizzled fur. It lay at my feet, unmoving.

The possum travels light, its little brain just a bit of spit and blood, poor synapses that can't recall where it slept the day before. It's nomadic, solitary, stopping here or there to sleep, to eat, and in the spring to mate. When cornered, it'll hiss and bare its teeth, and then commit its suicide. You think it's dead, and chances are it is, but when you leave it might wake up, sneer, and move along.

I looked up at the sky, almost as if to pray, but really because I didn't know what else to do. The sky was clear, and the stars crowded around the Milky Way, familiar and shimmering above our little group: me, the old Chevy, and the dead possum. Two mammals and a car.

I knew there had to be more I could do to forget, so I climbed over the guardrail, walked into the meadow bordering the road, found a level spot and lay down on my back.

The stars shifted and split into their familiar grid. These stars were the same dusty balls that Dad had pointed out to me and Joanna in our little backyard in Charleston, the same planets and constellations he'd taught me to map and magnify.

Lying there in the meadow, I focused in on just one cluster—the Pleiades—and stared. I forced myself not to blink, and willed the light of the stars to erase everything I knew about them and their company. To erase the nights I'd sat bent over books in the living room, the nights I'd taken Libby out to show her a blue planet hurtling toward us or a red one drifting away.

I stared until I thought I could see the Lost Pleiad, the seventh star in the constellation that the Greeks said hides from grief or shame. I willed its light to burn my memory out.

And then I shifted my focus in again, and the whole night sky filled my vision, and for just one second, it looked the way it had when I was a young child, before Dad started disappearing, before the fissure of adolescence, before I'd moved to Durham, and long before I'd ever heard of Libby Grant. For the briefest of moments, it was just the sky.

And then it all shifted back to the familiar grid, all the lines justified within their expected parameters.

I spread my arms wide, stood, and walked back to the car. The island was waiting, and by my calculations I'd be there soon. When I climbed over the guardrail, I looked around, but the possum was gone.

C O T T A G E

As the ferry plowed across the lake, I stood on the deck, my back leaning against the bulk of the Chevy, which took up more than its share of room. Slowly the mainland slipped down into the horizon, and for a long time we rode on uninterrupted water, no land fragmenting the swells, just the hollow slap of the waves against the steel hull. When I saw the island rise up out of the cold water, serene, isolated, and very still, I knew I had at last done something right.

With a metallic thud on the ramp, I drove the Chevy off the gangplank, and then kept going. There wasn't any decision to make about which road to take: just one road led away from the dock and into the green of the island.

One by one the other cars in the parade turned off, to stop at the little ice cream shack or to pull down some dirt road.

But I kept going. Beneath the sky, which felt rounded, more concave than I'd ever felt before, the island meadows unfurled in twin waves banking the black road. We slipped around the pastures, then crested a small rise, and there, spread out beneath me, lay the curve of the island's shoreline.

The weight of the Chevy plunged us both down the hill, into the heart of the island.

I didn't want to stop driving; I felt nearly happy in the Chevy, the window down, the lake-moist air lifting in the window.

But then I saw the sign, "Cottage for Rent," with an arrow pointing down an unpaved side road, and I turned down the road, surprised by how the lake appeared in the curve of each bend I rounded. Finally, a driveway with another, smaller sign, "Cottage."

I eased down the long drive lined with hosta lilies until I came to a weathered gray farmhouse. I parked next to a red pickup truck; as I walked up the flagstone path, I could glimpse a hint of the lake on the far side of the house. When I was about to knock on the door, a woman's voice said, "Finally warmed up, didn't it?"

She was walking around the side of the house, carrying a bunch of basil in one hand and a pair of clippers in the other. She was older than me, maybe around forty-five, and her face looked a little hard. She had a lot of sharp edges, her hair short and spiky, her shoulders a nearly straight line under her blue t-shirt.

"You must be here about the cottage. I'm Vivien," she said, taking off her gardening glove and wiping her brow. Her hands were lined with garden dirt.

"I'm Virginia. Virginia Didelphis," I said. How did she know why I'd come?

"Well, why don't you go on down to the cottage—it's over on the west shore. I've got to stay here to meet Ray. Here, I'll make you a map."

I followed her into a side door, which led into a kitchen papered with strawberry clusters marching repeatedly across the wall. Here, it seemed to fit.

She rummaged around in some papers until she found an old envelope and a stubby pencil, and she drew a little map with "LAKE" written on the sides of it and curvy lines to indicate the water.

"You won't need a key; I was just over there airing it out." She smiled as she handed me the paper, and I thought she didn't look so stern after all.

A clipped lawn aproned around the cottage, which sat in a cluster of wind-shortened white pines and rosebushes at the bottom of a straight dirt driveway. It wasn't the kind of place I ever would have chosen, with its green clapboards darkened with age and winter stains, its steep roof snowed under with brown pine needles.

I sat in the Chevy, leaned my forehead against the steering wheel, and wept. What was I doing here, anyway?

I was so far from home, and no one knew who I was, and it was all so different—the summer air cool and dry, the voices so fast, everyone a stranger to me.

I cried for a long time in the Chevy, and again the wish came through me: If only I could just call Libby and hear her say it had been a bad dream, that of course I was still her beloved, and wouldn't I please come home. Or maybe she would come for me here, to this purely preserved island. Couldn't she come find me?

When I lifted my head, I saw the lake's glimmer through the white pines. I got out of the car and walked toward the water, and stared over a rock ledge out at the blue expanse. I turned, and saw the screened porch facing the lake.

The screen door screeched when I opened it. On the porch, a red wicker table and chair with floral-print cushions faced out to the water. I sat in that chair, and looked out at the lake.

Maybe this lake was deep enough to hold everything, my rising fear, my memory, the sadness that lay coiled in my lungs.

I stood, and opened the glass door. Inside, the ceiling stretched up to its pitched pinnacle. The furniture was simple: a green cotton chaise and a mission rocker in one corner, and a small, square table of thick wood, with two stiff chairs, in the other. The walls were bare, just studs and the unpainted planks. A doorway led into a small bedroom, clean but dark, with a six-paned window looking lakeward and a single bed covered with a quilt of red-and-yellow-patchwork sailboats floating across a stitched sea of white.

My destiny: the single bed of the reformed sinner, with a nice view.

In the back of the house, I found a bathroom, and a kitchen with a white gas stove and a back door that looked over the little lawn.

I lay down on the floor of the high-ceilinged room, and thought of my possibilities. It suddenly seemed not to matter at all if I kept moving, or if I landed here at last.

A L I A S

I guess I've got good genes for this kind of thing, because it's come so easily for me: all the shifting, lying, hedging, dodging the truth.

Turning from my right hand to my left was easiest; maybe because I was desperate to take the emphasis from the hand that had written postcards and letters to Libby and that had touched her in love. I started by lifting my coffee cup with my left, and progressed to opening jars and pumping gas. When I moved into the cottage, I was careful to turn the doorknob with my left hand, and then writing left-handed just sort of followed.

The first time I really knew it was working was that first morning I woke in the cottage. I woke scared, unsure where I was in the old single bed in the dark little room, the summer light eking in between the wide boards of the plain wood walls. The room looked and smelled like a summer camp, the musty smell mingling with the detergent and bleach from the pillowcases and sheets Vivien had provided me.

I woke afraid, but more afraid of my nightmare than of being in such a strange place. In the dream I'd been watching a bus pull away from the curb, Libby's face pressed to the window, mouthing my old name. For a minute I believed in the power of dreams, and thought maybe Libby was searching for me somewhere. Maybe she'd come find me! But then I remembered the tag end of the dream: Doris' face in the bus window behind Libby, dwarfed by Libby's angular symmetry, smirking.

So there I was again; just another nightmare. I got up and walked out to the big lake-lit room of the cottage; I made some coffee on the gas stove, then sat in the red wicker porch chair with my coffee and a yellow legal pad and a pencil with "Ray's Feed and Antiques" stenciled on it which I'd found by the bed. From the porch, I could see the blue lake water and I could hear it moving against the shore.

I tore a sheet off the legal pad and then, without even thinking, took the pencil in my left hand and wrote.

> If a bus picked
> you up curbside and I was run-
> ning from a block away I'd get
> there just a moment too late,
> just as the bus was pulling out,
> smoking me out in its black

fumes, but I'd keep running,
I'd see your face pressed to the
window and your mouth fram-
ing my old name and I'd call
out, "WAIT," as I ran alongside, heedless of traffic on the
side streets or vendors with
their carts or barking dogs,
running along the city avenue,
but I wouldn't be alone, not
really, because you'd be in the
bus, riding along beside me,
standing as you neared the
next stop, descending from the
bus to take me in your arms,
weeping, exhausted, both of us
relieved down to our cells.

The words just came from my pen. I looked at them,
and they looked very different from my right-handed
writing. The letters were bumpier, almost like my grand-
mother's writing, but they were legible, certainly believ-
able. So it was easier than I'd thought it would be, and that's
what made me think maybe some of my father's genes
were passed on to me after all, as I had always feared.

I had thought about setting up a post office box for myself in Canada, so that Joanna, at least, could write to me.
But it was too close, even though I'd have to cross the border. My disappearance made me feel for the first time—
despite Libby's mistrust of me—that I had, after all,

inherited some of Dad's cunning. But if I had, then Joanna had certainly inherited our mother's gift for suspicion and detective work, and if I sent her an address at a Canadian P.O. box, she'd figure it out quickly enough.

When I'd been at her place in California in the spring, Joanna and I sat on her deck in the evenings after she got home from her job as a lab tech—she had found good use for those skills of precise documentation she'd learned as a girl. The sun glinted off the waters of the Pacific Ocean, and the little deck of her fourth-floor apartment seemed like a removed planet hovering above the blue.

Joanna herself was a little like a planet knocked off its orbit—removed from everything, so that we'd never been what you call close. On that visit, our orbits seemed to converge momentarily: a brief trine, and then apart. I'd gone out there not only to force myself to stop driving by Libby's house, but also because I wanted more answers about my own solitary spinning—the spinning that seemed to be at the core of why Libby was leaving me.

On Joanna's deck we'd talked about how Dad had assumed a second identity after I was born, when Joanna was three. He'd had a bank account in Savannah during the years we lived in Charleston, and he'd had a post office box there too. He thought we didn't know, and I hadn't, but Joanna and Mom did.

There were always hints and allegations, but they were oblique, avoidable. Somehow the child's mind calibrates for anything that's out of place. During that week with Joanna, and in the months that followed, the truth of Dad and Mom and our childhood became clear: my father had lived a double life, with his other woman and other friends, a P.O. box, and who knows, maybe other children, too.

It all fit in with his scheming, his inventions that were going to make us a million but which he abandoned: the basement was littered with telescope parts and plans and drawings for obscure astronomical devices.

Joanna's take on him was different from mine.

"He never had the self-esteem to finish anything. I mean, don't you think he felt terrible that he never got his Ph.D., that he was stuck teaching high school year after year?"

I shook my head no. "He could have gotten it. Maybe if he hadn't been so busy with Miss Gina Topsham"—I couldn't help drawing the name out sarcastically—"he could have gotten it." She looked at me, perplexed, and I wasn't sure if she'd worked everything out and now forgave him and was therefore farther along on the road to mental health than I was or if she still hadn't gotten out of the driveway.

"But you know," she said, wrinkling her brow in concentration, "his own parents did not encourage him. They were alcoholics, remember. Plus, Mom was so sick most of the time."

"But he lied to us. To all of us. For years."

Last fall, when Joanna first told me the details she knew, I thought, Aha. Now I can tell Libby that I know why I've been so removed. I'd hang up after talking with Joanna and find Libby in the living room. I wanted to say, Listen, this is starting to make sense, but then I'd feel the old fear mounting inside me, and more often than not I went mute.

Libby could so easily twist anything into proof that I didn't love her, and I didn't want to risk it.

After I visited Joanna in March, even though Libby by then was deeply involved with Doris, I'd been excited to think I could go back to Durham, and my new insight would make some difference, would bring Libby back.

But it didn't matter, by then. By that time I'd let Libby's jealousy of my friends, her insistence that I didn't love her, burn a hole right through us both. And I had no blanket to throw on the flames, no way of saying, simply, "You're just being ridiculous, let's talk about something interesting." And in the end, how like Dad Libby turned out to be, concealing her incipient romance with Doris, keeping me tethered to her with her declarations of love even as she started building her secondary, other life elsewhere.

No. I knew that if I wrote to Joanna, she'd find this island and make me go back to Durham, to see Dr. Israel again, and Dr. Israel would say that running from my pain would only prolong the recovery process.

There is no recovering. There's just the blue lake water, so cold and deep that it will pull the memory from me, the water level rising incrementally each time I dive in.

WALKING INTO WATER

It wasn't until I'd gotten all settled in at the cottage that I
realized the island was ideal for amnesia exercises. I still
had the page I'd torn from *Wescott and Williamson's* in that
library; in fact, I'd hung it from a nail that was poking out
of the living room wall. It was my only decoration.

I reread it: " ... transient global amnesia sometimes
results from emotional trauma, travel in a motor vehicle,
immersion in hot or cold water, or increased cerebrovascular flow."

Well. I'd certainly done the travel in a motor vehicle
and the emotional trauma. But I knew it was the water that
held the most promise for blotting out my memory.

That evening I climbed down the wooded path to the
beach, such as it was. There was no sand; I didn't think
there was any on the whole island, just these great slabs of

black rock. The cliffs that hung above the beach were made up of flinty layers—I could see how the layers were compressed, one on top of the other. I wondered if the whole island was like that.

The water looked completely different from southern water. It was a flat, bright blue, and very clear, even in the fading light. There wasn't any wind, and I could see the reflection of the pines and the cliffs making a mirror upside-down world in the water, a world where everything would be different.

I stood there in my cutoffs and a white t-shirt and my blue sneakers. I could see the shore of the isthmus, just an indistinct rim of green dotted with white specks that could have been other shoreline cottages. Above the green there hung a strip of yellow light, then a line of purple fading into blue sky, going darker and darker as I tipped my head back.

I tilted my head upright again, watching the sky go from dark to light, and then I started walking. I was shocked by the first snap of cold around my ankles. But I kept going, the icy water rising around me with each step I took, bloating my shorts till they floated around my legs, filling my t-shirt till it ballooned to the surface, then slapped down silently against my wet skin. I took a deep breath, and kept walking, the water rising over my head, my hair spilling out around me, then washing around my face, till I thought my lungs would burst, and then I released the breath, allowing my arms and legs to just drag and billow and lift, and while the air rushed from my lungs and my body floated to the surface, I just kept saying to myself: Forget, forget, forget.

Forget what? The cold swells rose around me, washing up through my limbs and porous skin, macerating my tired memory. Let it seep up my spine and through my skull, washing out my recollection, drowning all that rests nestled deep in my brain.

STATIONER'S

The old stationer's store in the mainland city sat on the corners of Main, Rue du Lac, and St. Frederick, in one of those triangular buildings that appear to be optical illusions, exercises in perspective for drawing students, or architects' ways of working out their feelings of mathematical superiority. It looked like the building in Charleston where Mom's insurance agent had his office. We'd go in there on a hot afternoon, and he'd let me play with his terrific collection of varied rubber stamps: cars and traffic lights and trains, the stuff that made up the tedium of insurance claims for him, but which afforded me the joy of sitting in the big leather chair, the fan blowing air toward my face, while he and Mom discussed her options.

When I saw this stationer's on the triple corner in the mainland city, I was drawn to it, tugged toward the marble steps, wanting to add my own weight to the weight of the thousands who had worn down indentations in the marble like twin riverbeds just waiting for the stream.

Inside, the place smelled like the old dry goods shop that I went to when I was a kid. I loved that feeling of being on the verge, of the optimistic anticipation the trip would bring: Mom chatting with the shopgirl while Joanna and I compared notebooks and pencils. When I was ten, Mom bought me a special present, a wooden pencil box with a picture of four birds perched on a branch on the plastic front. The little drawer slid out of the box, like a secret hiding place.

What I loved when I was a kid was the promise I always hoped would prove true in those September shopping trips: maybe *this* year the chaos of our house would somehow fall to order, if Joanna and I could keep our books organized and neat: we'd all have dinner together at six every night, and Dad and Mom would read in the tidy living room all evening, while Joanna and I worked out math problems and vocabulary lists on our clean sheets of paper. We'd know where to find things, and our lives would have a frame, a grid like the grid on the graph paper, where all the fear could be penned in.

This stationer's smelled like that one: graphite and newsprint and reams of clean paper. I walked up the aisle, the wooden floorboards creaking under my feet. In the dim light I could make out the rows of supplies: tiny square cardboard boxes of paper clips, fish-mouthed jars of clean-cut pencils with their brand-new erasers, copy paper and legal pads and notebooks, all precisely stacked, waiting at attention.

It was the notebooks that gave me the idea of another step I could take toward amnesia. It was clear by now that I had to reinvent myself, to imagine myself amnesiac. The person who'd loved Libby was not able to brook the nightmarish bodily truth that Libby was gone, evaporated into another person, a person who slept and woke with Doris. The woman who'd canoed with Libby so many dawns, laughing and shushing as she passed the thermos across the hull, the woman who'd waited on the beach for the little dot of Libby to become real, that woman had to die, because she couldn't live as witness to such depletion. And if I couldn't bring myself to take the required number of pills, at least I could attempt the creation of someone else, someone who would never miss that safe little pencil box with the birds on it or the slow width of North Carolina. Or Libby. Someone who had never known what I'd known with her.

So I picked up one of the blank books with the stiff blue covers. I let it fall open to the natural part. I liked the off-white paper and the big numbers printed in the upper corner on each page. I took it up to the counter.

"I'd like to open a charge account," I told the woman at the old manual cash register.

She tore a sheet from a pad. "Just write your name and address, and sign on the bottom," she said.

I did, scratching out the long scrawl I'd first signed back at the motel, and then I crossed the creaking wooden planks back out to the marble steps.

AMNESIAC'S JOURNAL

The light as we
near five a.m. lifts the island's
objects from amnesia of night
into memory's sly catch. The
first morning bird lets out two
notes, and the willow, silvered
now, now greening, and the
pines come into sharp relief
against the rosing, bluing sky.

Amnesiac, I watch the
grassy lawn appear, inimitable
rosebush and the tiger lilies
pressing up from shadows into
light.

The meadow's curve rises

from the dark side of Amnesia
into dawn, sky paling with the
light of memory.

The willow twigs that
hang, shuffling from the
branch's nest, like tendrils,
tentative, make a filigree of
still-forgotten black against the
bluing sky.

Far off on meadow's edge,
the silhouettes of stubby island
cedars rise, and then the cows
appear, plodding through their
pasture in a straight-backed
line of certainty.

G R O C E R Y

As soon as the glass doors slid open and I stepped into the mainland supermarket, I missed home in a way I hadn't before.

A supermarket is an intimate place, and the Winn-Dixie in Durham and I had grown very close to one another. I would come swinging in, in one motion swerve a cart into the produce section, then make my way, confident, knowledgeable, through the store. I even knew some of the checkers by name.

I walked into this store, and was immediately scared, scared at how unfamiliar it was. And then I remembered how, on our few tandem forays to the Winn-Dixie, Libby would toss me the apples and oranges and chat with the guy at the fish counter, making him laugh at something. And then I was glad to be here, in a market where I recognized nothing.

I pushed my cart along, not really looking for the familiar names and colors on the boxes, but gradually realizing that the names were different here. There were no boxes of hominy grits or Ruth Sprague's Soups or shelves of various tobacco products. Here, some of the names were even in French.

I put things in the cart, anyway. I selected the usual—detergent and sponges, and bananas and apples, chicken and coffee and eggs. I made my way around to the ice cream, and pulled out a pint of chocolate.

When I turned, I put the ice cream in the cart, then started pushing along; but as I pushed and looked down at my food, I realized that it wasn't my food at all, and for a minute, I thought that the amnesia exercises were working after all, and a terror flooded through me, and I looked back, and saw the cart, the cart that had been mine, abandoned, standing with its bananas and chicken and cleaning supplies. From this end of the aisle, I could see that I'd put in a packet of the mint cookies Libby always liked.

I looked into the cart I'd mistaken for my own. The things in it weren't all that unusual: bacon, potatoes, shredded wheat. A package of frozen spinach. A bag of pretzels. But the fact that someone else had selected them, that they were part of another person's life, familiar in a northern household somewhere, expected, loved, made them seem almost tainted, and my inadvertent theft of the cart seemed criminal.

I thought of the depth of the water, imagined slicing into the taut surface of the lake, my hands folded above my head, and I pushed the cart, this stranger's food chosen by a stranger, up to the checkout counter, and paid.

ACCIDENT

At Sandy's Snack Shack that July Sunday, they were giving away free soft-serves to everyone: to all the accident victims who hadn't been taken away by the ambulance, the cops and the ambulance attendants, and even, as I had hoped they would, to the curious or maudlin onlookers.

I used to be very good about not stopping to look at accidents. Part of it was that I just didn't want to see something awful—on the few occasions when I did glance surreptitiously at a wreck, I always, selfishly, thought of myself. I imagined that it was me looking helplessly up from the stretcher. The worst accident I saw was on my way to the lab at Beaufort one time when the cops had to stop the traffic just as I arrived at the intersection, and I could see the face of the woman who was lying crumpled up a little in the driver's seat of the smashed car. She was waiting for the Jaws of Life machine to wrench her car door off so she could go to the emergency room only to learn, probably, that she was dying of some slow-moving disease anyway.

But the other reason I never used to stop, and this was probably more of a deciding factor, was that I wanted the cops to like me. I didn't want them laughing at me on their coffee break. I wanted to be a good girl about it, and respect the fact that the police were having a hard enough time at a terrible accident without yet another person insisting on looking tragedy in the face.

So I was glad in a way that I came across the accident at Sandy's Snack Shack. I mean, accidents do happen, and I wasn't glad that people had been hurt and their everyday lives all torn up, but I was glad that if there had to be an accident that day, at least I came across it in time.

I was glad because now that I'd vanished, now that I was obliterating my former self, on this sole surviving summer island, where there are no fast-food places or movie theaters or superhighways or fax machines, now that I was here, I could do anything I wanted. I'd trained myself to become left-handed, to take my coffee black, and even, if the whim hit me, to not only slow down at the scene of an accident but come to a full stop, pull my car over, get out, and watch.

And with a free chocolate-vanilla swirl to boot.

So I sat on the redwood picnic table, my feet on the bench, licking my ice cream and watching the ambulance attendants bandage up a middle-aged man's arm. Their ice cream, in dishes, sat on the pavement. I watched the state police trooper in his trim gray-blue uniform sitting at the next picnic table over, interviewing one of the girls who works at Sandy's.

"She must have seen the whole thing," a woman's voice near me said, and I turned around and saw a large woman, about my age, in a floral dress. She had a vanilla swirl cone in one hand, and a little boy clutched at her other hand. He had two fingers in his mouth.

"Do you know what happened?" I asked, and felt I could be asking about anything in the world: Do you know what happened to cause this accident, or do you know what happened to begin the generation of cells that led to life on the planet, or do you know what happened to me, that I moved to this strange place?

She just shook her head.

By the time I'd finished my ice cream, the ambulance was pulling away, and the cop was putting his notebook in his back pocket, and the technician was measuring the last skid mark. The girl from Sandy's was back behind the counter with Sandy and as I walked back to my car I could hear them talking about which cop they thought was the cutest.

H A I R

I've always been afraid of waking up one morning, putting
my hand behind my head, and realizing that my hair had
somehow been shorn off while I slept. In fifth grade the
boys would tease me, threatening my two braids with scis-
sors, till finally Mrs. Markley let me sit in the back row. I
liked it better back there, anyway; I could just prop my chin
in my hands and dream.

    Other than that fear, I'd never thought of cutting it
short. Like plastic surgery, or breast implants, or taking
pills to make me taller, it's just never seemed an option.
Plus, Libby was wild about my hair. "I knew that when I finally found you, you'd be beautiful, but I never knew you'd
have this pelt," she said a coupe of months after we got together. She called it brushing my fur, when we'd sit together on the front porch, *The Washington Post* on my lap,

Libby sitting one step above me, brushing, then braiding, her long legs spraddled on either side of me.

One time she took close-ups of my hair, magnifying it so many times that it looked like the curling strands of zooplankton under the microscope. Cutting my hair off seemed like a good way to fulfill the requirement of emotional stimuli for an attack of transient global amnesia.

When I first read the description in *Wescott and Williamson's*, I thought I'd had about as many emotional stimuli as a person can stand without hurling herself and her Chevy over the cliff's edge, but being here on this island had calmed me down. Some nights I didn't even have the nightmares anymore, and on those nights, I'd wake feeling soothed by the lake water. Then, often, I'd remember that my waking life was really the nightmare; still, I was beginning to have those moments when I'd feel all right.

And that's how I ended up with a pink plastic robe draped around me, my palms wetting the chair arms under the plastic, slightly sickened by the smell of permanent solutions and hair sprays and by what I was about to do.

In the mirror, I looked like I was just a head stuck on top of a big pink triangle.

The hairdresser, who said her name was Marlo, after Marlo Thomas, was very skinny, and short even in her spike heels. "No bigger than a minute," Libby would have said, and next to Libby's rangy height, she would have looked like a doll, in her fashionably patterned tights and short yellow dress. I could just see Libby leaning against the mirror, one elbow draped over the top.

Forget it, I told myself.

The hairdresser's own hair was teased up in a kind of modified bouffant, a cross between Gina Lollobrigida and Elvis Presley.

"Are you sure you want to do this?" she asked. "It's an awfully dramatic change. And you have *great* hair." She took a big chunk of it in one hand and squeezed it for emphasis.

"Oh, I'm sure," I said. "It's just not me anymore."

It took her a long time, and the whole time that she was cutting, I just stared at my own eyes in the mirror, without blinking. I focused and focused in, until my mirror-pupils got bigger and bigger. By the time the hairdresser was done, I could hardly see.

"There you go," she sighed. "I hope this is really what you wanted."

I blinked to bring the world back to order.

I couldn't help the little shock of misrecognition I felt when I looked at my image in the mirror, the whole image, not just the eyes. But I'd prepared myself, and immediately made myself think, You've always looked like this.

Marlo untied the pink plastic robe, and when I stood up, I saw the hair lying around the chair in a semicircle, like the shed pelt of a strange mammal, something northern and hibernal, something used to living in the cold.

I've always thought the mustelids—minks and martens and weasels—are a little evil, with their thick fur and tiny black eyes and short legs and scent glands musking up their dens. Even the river otters seem a little dangerous. But with my shorn hair, I felt sleek, like an obligate water mammal, like a carnivore with big canine teeth yellowed by slicing sinew and sucking up muddy water.

That night I waited until after dark to go into the water. I felt more nocturnal, too, with my short hair. I picked my way down the steep path.

Down by the water, the sky was wide, stretched out over the lake, and lighter than it was up by the cottage. The night wind was up, pushing the water into waves that rolled in from way out where the eels slip by.

I pulled my t-shirt off over my head, waiting for the collar to catch on my heavy braid, then realizing the braid was gone. I unbuttoned my shorts and let them drop, and kicked off my sneakers. For a moment I was afraid someone would see me, even though there were just the rock cliffs, and the tiny lights of the isthmus far off the shore. And anyway, I felt invisible.

This time, instead of walking straight into the water and gradually submerging my body and my memories and everything, I walked up to where the breakers were coming in. They were small, and I let a couple pound against my bare knees.

I took a deep breath, inhaling the northern night air, the ambient damp darkness. I folded my arms straight above my head, and dove into the shallow water, feeling my breasts and stomach graze against the flat sheets of rock.

"Nothing ever happened," I sang to myself, and then I sang it in what I imagine to be the language of mustelids, with the dark water singing all around me, the eels and trout and salmon near my legs, swimming beside me, all of us glowing in the dark night water.

BIRTHDAY

They say it's bad luck to cry on your birthday; but then, how could my luck get any worse? Besides, this was my old birthday, and nobody knew it; at least, no one I was in contact with.

I'd decided to spend the day like any other, although all week I kept noticing the date—an announcement for a strawberry supper or fishing derby or even just the calendar kept catching my eye.

But as with everything else, I told myself it wasn't really a part of my life—that this particular day had no meaning to me now.

I even realized that although I'd have to make up a new birthday for myself—it always comes up in conversation eventually—I didn't have to adhere to it. I could say November 12th or February 20th or April 6th, and then as the month approached, I was sure no one would really remember.

I knew enough not to make it too near a national or re ligious holiday.

On this day, I knew it was my original birthday, and I knew that one year ago Libby was waking me with a big mug of creamy coffee and a bowl of glazed fruit, preparing to load the canoe onto the Land Rover and pile our beach gear, the books and the camera and the picnic and me onto the seats.

But today was just another day, and I'd forget. All the gifts she'd given me over the years, the little toys, the postcards, and the clay animals from Italy, were slowly decaying in their boxes in North Carolina.

I was glad, because I could fall backward only too easily into melancholia and haul out the presents and cards from one year ago, or two, or three, and pretend that she'd given them to me today.

I found myself wondering when Doris' birthday is— she must have one—and has it gone by yet, and what gift did Libby give her? How did she wake her, and from what dreams?

But instead of all that, I pictured the things in storage, evaporating. I imagined the mold creeping over them, covering the whole jumble that I'd dumped into the cardboard cartons on January 2. I saw the coffee cup with the rose-twined ceramic handle, and the valentines, and the cat hand puppet lying facedown, and imagined the irreversible breakdown of their molecular structure. I thought of the whole box just falling to chaos and then evaporating.

And then I poured myself another cup of coffee, which I've learned to brew very strong. It makes me feel robust, the way a shot of scotch used to.

The radio station that scratches in from the mainland played a recording of Beethoven's Ninth; I listened straight through, looking out at the water.

In the evening, I lit my kerosene lantern and hung it on the porch. I walked down to the lake, and dove in like it was some kind of baptism.

DINNER

I pulled down the driveway to the cottage one evening, the pine trees a stiff and serious fence hemming the Chevy along the narrow drive. I was tired; that day I'd driven across the island and taken the ferry over to Canada, where I bore the burden of the outsider, stretching for French words I didn't understand, trying to make out the price of a sandwich or the directions at the *station-service* for filling the Chevy's thirsty tank.

It was good to be in a country where everyone spoke a language that I had never spoken with Libby. I wondered if this was how the amnesiac feels when she first wakes, that sounds just float out from people's mouths, and their lips move.

When I got out of the Chevy and started up the path to the cottage, at first I wasn't sure what the patch of white on the door was: sunlight, or some scrap of refuse that blew there and then got stuck? And then I realized it was a note—a note from Libby! At last—and I bounded to the door, hands trembling, and touched it, right where it was, stuck with a silver tack sunk deep into the soft wood of the cottage door.

Libby.

I traced the border of the note, then, fingers trembling, popped the tack out and lifted it, for a moment, to my cheek. I inhaled, wanting to smell her familiar scent. Of course it just smelled like paper, but that was okay. Briefly, I wanted to cherish the note, to wait before unfolding it, anticipation building. But I was too anxious, too relieved to pause, and I unfolded the paper in one quick snap.

I saw at once that the note wasn't written in Libby's angular, sometimes illegible, scrawl; instead, the letters sloped forward in a shaky script. But my desire for it to be from her persisted, even in the face of reason: I wondered why she was disguising her handwriting, and why she began with "Virginia," instead of with my own old name. I was confused, even though I knew the note couldn't be from her, wasn't from her. I felt that old panic that had tangled me up as a child when I couldn't make sense of Dad's absences, the same bewilderment I'd felt when Libby told me she was leaving.

I looked quickly at the signature: "Vivien Marquette."

Of course. Even though I'd known the note couldn't be from Libby, I was still stunned, feeling the loss as if it were fresh. I sat down hard right there on the shale front step, and when I finally looked up, the pasture across the driveway was fading into evening blue; the Holsteins in a line plodded barnward, toward their comforting hay and stanchions. I stood, letting the note drop from my lap to the ground, and walked down the ledge to the water.

The shore lay motionless beneath the deepening blue sky, just a single line of yellow light stripped along the horizon. I scanned the lake, looking for a sail, a sail ruddered by Libby's competent hands.

But no. It won't happen like that, I told myself; it may not happen at all. I walked into the still water, feeling it rise around me until my legs and torso and then my shoulders were submerged. I stood like that for a long time, letting my arms drift up from my sides to the water's surface. Then I plunged under, and as I swam, my mind emptied of Libby, or the hope, or the relief. I swam until I couldn't remember even her handwriting.

When I was done swimming, I floated on my back under the lake's rounded sky-bowl, wondering what I would do if Libby did come for me. It was preposterous: no one knew where I was. But if she did, would I want to leave my cottage and canoe and lake? Would I relinquish everything I'd found?

Shivering up to the cottage door, my wet clothes clinging to me like some terrible reptililan skin, I picked up the note, and read: "Virginia—Would you like to come by the house for dinner one night this week? Any night is fine; I usually eat around six or so. I hope everything is working out for you. Best, Vivien Marquette."

I went into the cottage, dropped my wet clothes in the kitchen sink, stood under the hot shower spray, then put on my sweatshirt and shorts. I picked up the note again—it was becoming less and less affiliated with Libby—and impaled it on a nail that pierced from the wall, opposite the wall where I'd hung the page from *Wescott and Williamson's*.

On Friday, when I finally showed up at Vivien's, it was all less difficult than I'd feared. I found my way easily on the simple island roads, meadows plunging to the water, and then I nosed the Chevy up the curving driveway, pocketing the bay bends, till I saw the weathered gray clapboards.

I parked behind Vivien's red pickup truck, got out, and looked around. The flowers clustered against the house seemed bushier than I'd remembered, and the view of the lake I could make out from the side of the house seemed to stretch wider. I walked up the brick path to the back door; before I had a chance to knock, I heard Vivien call out through the screen, "Hey, is that Virginia? Come on in."

I opened the door and stepped in. Vivien was standing at the old white porcelain sink, pouring a steaming pot of something into a blue colander. The kitchen wasn't as old-farmhousey as I'd thought; new, light-grained wood cabinets stood at the walls, topped with clean white counters.

"I'm glad you finally decided to come by," Vivien said. I was a little unnerved by the way her look seemed to go right through me; I was afraid, suddenly, that she'd try to get some information out of me.

"Thanks for inviting me," I said quickly.

As it turned out, she didn't ask me much at all, at least

not about why I'd come here or what I'd done for work, that sort of thing. Instead, she brought grilled lake salmon and salad out to the front porch, and we sat at her wrought-iron table looking out over the lake, and she told me about the island, how she came here ("My god, it's nearly ten years ago now") after she quit drinking. She told me how she'd worked in Alaska at a fish-packing plant, chopping heads off salmon, till the fifteen-hour nights and the stench of blood and gills and scales got to her, and she was finally drinking more than working.

"God, it was wonderful," she said, laughing. "Wonderful and terrible, I mean."

I almost told her how I quit drinking too, five years ago, when Mom died of breast cancer. I wanted to tell Vivien how I now thought that the cancer cells must have been generated by Mom's longing, her despair; how it seems to me that the center of her cells must have absorbed her grief and so split haphazardly, propelling all the other cells into confusion and hysteria. Luckily, I caught myself in time, and just nodded and asked her how she had come to the island.

"Sometimes I think I must have imagined this island into existence; on days when I believe I have some supernatural power that other human beings couldn't possibly possess, I think that. But looking back, it was more mundane than that: I wanted quiet, and someplace strikingly beautiful, and water. My family used to vacation here summers, so it was a natural choice."

Once I realized Vivien wasn't about to ask me anything about myself—out of polite respect for my privacy or simple self-centeredness, I still wasn't sure—I began to like the way she looked at me intently as we talked. It calmed me down, so that when I left I felt relaxed, the way I felt after a long swim.

On the way home, I rolled down the Chevy's heavy window, and I could hear the metallic racket of the red-winged blackbirds. Along the roadside, a rabbit darted into the long meadow grasses, then another, as I rounded the bends of the island's inlets.

J O B

The money I'd taken from our accounts and that I'd gotten
for the Toyota was lasting me longer than I had thought it
would: the cottage was cheap, and other than food, I didn't
have many expenses.

But then I saw the ad in the island paper: "Diver
Wanted." I wondered what kind of job this could be, up
here. I left the paper folded open to the ad, on the wicker
porch table for a couple of days. Every time I'd go out there,
I'd read it again: "Diver Wanted. Inquire at Plummer and
Joaillier Marina." Not much for me to mull over, not exactly
a plethora of words from which to eke some kind of meaning, from which to envision activities that would fill my
days, from which to create fantasies of moving through
water. There weren't even very many letters that I could
play into anagrams.

On the third day, I took the ferry over to the mainland, then drove along Harbor Boulevard. If I come across the marina, I'll go in and ask about the job, I told myself. But when I saw it, the red-lettered sign, the little white clapboard building, my chest got that tight feeling again. What if they asked for my references? What if they wanted a Social Security number, a diving license? What if they wanted to know who I was?

I got out of the Chevy, and patted its roof. When I entered the dim room, I was careful not to let the screen door slam behind me, and for a second I wondered if I should have paid more attention to my clothes—I'd gotten accustomed to just pulling on whatever shorts and t-shirt were near my bed. My god, I thought, I want this job.

The man at the counter turned to me. He didn't look quite old enough to be working. "I'm here about the job, the diving job," I said, hoping he wouldn't catch the southern slope that still eased down on my voice.

"Oh yeah, Bill Withers' job. Hang on." He turned around, and lifted the microphone on an old two-way radio. "Withers lives out on Gull Isle. He wants someone to clean his boat hulls," he said as he scratched the radio on and handed me the microphone. "Just push that button when you talk, then let go," he said.

Soon a voice boomed over the microphone: "Gull Isle five-nine-six-four, over."

"Uh, hi. I'm here at the marina, calling about the diving job," I said, embarrassed at how shaky my voice sounded.

"That's great. Listen, first of all, since we're on the

radio, you have to say 'over' after you talk, do you read me, over?"

"Sure, no problem, over," I said. I hadn't spoken so quickly, without planning my words, in a very long time.

"I need someone to clean the hulls of my sailboats. It'd mean scraping underwater for a couple of weeks. They're anchored there at the marina. Would you know how to do that kind of work, over?"

"Sure. I've cleaned plenty of hulls. But I don't have my diving gear with me, over."

"That's okay, just tell Jeff there that you're working for me, and he'll set you up. I'll pay you half to start and half when you finish. Do you want it in a check or cash, over?"

"Um, cash, I guess would be better, over."

"Okay. Listen, I'll set it all up with Jeff, and you just come in sometime later this week, okay? And you can reach me on this radio anytime. So if that's all, this is Gull Isle, over and out."

I handed the microphone back to Jeff. He pushed on the red button. "Over and out," he said.

SNAKE

It was the snake, the snake and my reaction to it, that made me question how well the amnesia exercises were working. Although I missed Libby, I thought about her with less and less frequency. But when I saw the snake, I remembered that time when I was out mowing the lawn in Durham, and the memory forced me to consider a possibility I'd been dodging, that maybe I was better off here, alone, on this unfamiliar island.

That time, late last summer, Libby was away at a newspaper conference, and I found that I'd forgotten what it was like to come home near dark, struggling with keys and grocery sacks. I'd forgotten how the top of one bag inevitably rips just as you get to the door; how cold and still the inside of a house looks when you see it's undisturbed, just as you left it, only darker.

Toward the end of that week Libby was away, I was really beginning to question what had been in my mind when I insisted she go alone.

"I could use some time to myself," I'd told her.

Now, I had plenty of time to myself, time to think about how for so much of my life I've been alone, sunk deep in the center of my own protective concentric rings. When I was a little girl, I'd slip out the back door, drift away from the stultifying silence or the noisy arguments swirling in the house. I'd lie back on one of the lawn chairs and stare out over the backyard, adrift in my thoughts, our fat tabby cat curled on my lap.

I could see now how I was removed from Libby, or at least how she'd seen it that way. It wasn't so much that I wanted to be alone as that I just didn't know how to push myself out from my cozy self-protective covering. And isn't that what had attracted Libby to me, the dreamy way I'd drift off? Isn't that what magnetized us, that we were each floating in our own dream world, each unreachable?

The time with the snake in Durham, I was wishing I hadn't told Libby to go by herself; I was feeling lonely when on Thursday evening I came home early from work and got the mower out of the garage. I checked the gas, then poured in a little more, and pulled sharply on the cord.

There's something about mowing that always called forth a melancholy rush of memory in me. Maybe it was the meditative concentric circles, or pushing the weight of the mower against the slope of lawn; maybe it was the grasshoppers springing up in the path of the mower's deep approach, or the summer nearing twilight and the bugs and

the childhood smell of gasoline and grass; the swallows dipping down to catch the bugs that spray out behind the
wheels' deep tracks.

Whatever it was, I was in it, sunk deep into the steady
process of mowing, smelling the grass and gasoline, and
suddenly there was the snake spitting out from the blade's
underside. Just a green and brown and yellow twisting,
writhing ribbon, slit from the mower onto a heap of newly
shredded grass.

I stopped, but didn't scream. I knew it was too late for
that. I just stood there, the metal handle vibrating under
my hands, my mouth agape, the swallows dipping around
me.

I switched off the mower and dragged it back to the
garage. It was almost dark; the laundry I'd done the day before hung white in sharp relief against the sky. I got the
shovel out, and down by the linden tree I dug a hole. Then
I scooped the snake onto the shovel, carried it over, dropped
it in. I covered it up, then knelt down, and thought about
how unpredictable everything is, unpredictable and terrible
and fascinating. I missed Libby more in that moment than
I'd missed her all week, but I knew I couldn't tell her about
the snake over the phone; there was something too intimate
about it, so I'd have to wait, but by the week's end, the
freshness of the snake's death would have turned to something else, and Libby would never truly hear of this singular experience.

I went inside and turned on all the lights. I picked up
the photo of her I like best—the one where she's smirking
at me from her wicker chair on the porch of our house. For

a while I played around with the knot-tying kit she'd given me. I made a slipknot, and a three-way tieback, and a fisherman's loop.

That night I wore her blue cotton sweater to bed, and dreamt about water.

But this snake was different. No. The snake was the same kind, a little skinny ribbon snake, but with a velvety black back instead of the reddish brown. But more important, *I* was different: even if the amnesia wasn't taking hold as much as I'd wished, I knew I'd changed.

The day I saw the snake, I looked up from my breakfast—by then I'd taken to really making breakfast for myself—and there it was, coiled on the kitchen floor in a little circle, wound up like the innermost circle in the circles of lines I once mowed on our lawn.

It lay utterly still. I could see its skin was like braid, like braided yellow, black, and green threads. When I peered more closely, I could see a little pulse along the side of its neck. I opened my mouth and screamed, pressing my hands back behind me.

I screamed a long time. I dropped my head into my hands and screamed, remembering the other snake, remembering how I hadn't called Libby at her hotel that night. Remembering what she told me when she got home. How I never got the chance to tell her about the snake, because when she returned from the conference she said maybe she couldn't stay with me, and then we were in one discussion after another, my confusion escalating each time we'd talk. How she said I was too walled off from her, and she couldn't stand it, she had to be close to someone. How after that, I called Joanna weekly, twice weekly, pulling from her the long and tangled rope of truth that had lassoed our girlhood, as if unknotting everything in my past would provide me with some threshold revelation that would, in turn, allow me to open my heart more to Libby.

But what about Libby? Why did she say nothing of how remote *she* was, how she allowed her suspicion that I didn't love her to wedge us farther and farther from one another?

In those weeks I often thought of that snake, and wanted so much to tell her about it, how each of its many vertebrae attaches to a pair of muscles, how the muscles make a fabric allowing for motion. I wanted to tell her how the snake's jawbones are analogous to our ear ossicles, how closely related we are.

When I opened my eyes, I saw that the snake was moving, essing its way across the floor and then under the sofa. I had no idea where it would end up.

Maybe one day it will find its way into my bed. Maybe even now it's lying coiled in Libby's blue sweater which I tossed off during the night. Maybe tonight when I pull the sweater on, the snake will drop out into the bleached white sheets, wrap around my leg or arm, emit a hiss, and sleep.

C A N O E

Sometime early in August I found the canoe. It was on one of those nights when I was just driving around in the old Chevy—I had the window down and Sarah Vaughan was singing on the radio, and I rounded a bend I'd never rounded before, and there, nailed to a tree, was a little sign painted green with white letters: "Canoes for Sale or Rent."

I stopped the car. In the shadowy dark of the clouded stars, I could see three big hulks looming around on a lawn, and behind them a dark little house. I walked up to the smallest canoe.

It was white, and very small, and I could see where it had been patched in a couple of spots, the patches yellow now and rough, like patches of old alligator skin on the side of sleek snake.

As I stood there in the dim light, I saw Libby in the

front of that canoe we'd rented, passing me the thermos with her long reach. How I loved her surprise when the moose rose up from the cold water, how in that moment she was like a young girl, bewildered and brave at once.

And then I remembered how she'd stopped speaking to me that night, didn't speak the whole next day, after I told her how I'd learned to canoe years before, with Bridget in college. How I'd tried to cajole her that night, how I'd pleaded with her, and then how the questions she asked started to seem real to me, started to crowd up my thoughts: Was I really betraying Libby with my memories of Bridget? Should I somehow not remember her?

I ran my hand along the canoe's hull. In the half-light of the deep island night, it was like an animal, a reptilian mammal, a therapsid at long last springing back to life after 200 million years of extinction.

The next morning I walked over to the house, and there was a man in the yard sanding a big green Old Town, and I bought the little canoe. He helped me slip it into the water, and I put one foot in, then pushed off with the other. The canoe and I wobbled a little at first, but then we steadied and I paddled us out into the lake.

All those days of canoeing with Libby were finally paying off, I thought as the shore slipped quickly away. I felt confident and sure, and I remembered the first time we'd gotten into a canoe together, and how, paddling behind her into the deep wilderness of the Neuse River, I'd been so happy, watching the wings of Libby's scapulae moving beneath her white t-shirt.

I dug the paddle into the clear water of this northern

lake. That night at Blue Lake in Minnesota, we'd had dinner at the lodge dining room, and I'd told her about how Bridget and I had learned to canoe together, and as I was getting to the really funny part, I realized she was just staring out the big window at the sunset. Not eating. Mad.

So I'd done it again, said the words that would spin her inexorably down into her vortex of anger.

"Why do you feel compelled to tell me about all the other people you were with?" she asked, and I had no answer. I looked down at my plate, the confusion fogging around my head.

Toward the end, Libby got madder, more easily, and by then, I was questioning everything. Why did I tell her these things? Was it wrong of me? Or was it worse to not tell, and then to be lying to her? Was I doomed to be like Dad, thinking of someone else secretly? But these were innocuous memories, the stuff that made up my life. Then why did that cold fear creep into me? She thought it all went to prove that I didn't really love her: "If you really loved me, you wouldn't be afraid," she'd say as we lay not touching in the wide bed.

I dug the paddle into the water, turned, and saw the shore with my cottage up on a thin line of green, painted above a thicker wedge of gray shale. I stood in the canoe, and then knelt so I could see over the side.

The water was very deep, and very clear. I could see the Eurasian milfoil waving its long, leafy arms toward me; a fat silver fish slinked under the boat. Far, far down, I could make out rocks, lamellated with lake mud.

This is what it had been like, leaning over the edge last

winter, right before Libby left. I'd dived into the murky waters of the past, dived in to find the reasons I'd always felt such terror.

"It's no wonder I've been so afraid," I'd said to her. "Come on, for thirty-one years I believed my father was one person, and now I find out that my suspicions were right all along, and it turns out he really was the fabulous deceiver I'd always feared."

I doubt I would have sought out the full—or fuller, anyway—story of my parents' lives if it weren't for Libby. Even as I sat in that lodge dining room, the water of Blue Lake receding into the evening, terrified, confused, desperate, I knew that somehow all this business of jealousy and possession that seemed to ensnare me and Libby was in part the continuing diffusion of my childhood, as if the gases released twenty, thirty years ago were continuing to disperse.

But by then, she said, it was just too late. By then, the skin of my self-protection had formed an impenetrable bubble around me. And like an immune system attacked by a virus, my own defenses had turned on me.

I focused on my reflection. How much I'd wanted her to be waiting in the boat when I returned from those terrible waters, reaching her strong hand out to pull me, shivering with the truth, from the depths of childhood. How, in the end, she hadn't waited.

I focused on my reflection in the cold northern waters until I could see nothing else. I thought of the page from *Wescott and Williamson's* pinned to my cottage wall.

I dove in headlong off the canoe's rim and right into my own face, the boat barely rocking with my departure.

F I S H

I liked the salmon Vivien cooked for our dinner so much
that she gave me a booklet to read—*Salmon of the North
Atlantic*—and told me where to find a fishing rod and reel
and wicker tackle box, tucked away in the toolshed by the
cottage.

I loaded up the canoe and shoved off from shore, then
paddled to the center of the lake, feeling more weighted
and purposeful than I had on any of my previous canoe
glides. Once I found a spot that seemed to hover above
the deepest and coldest waters, I cast out my line and let the
bobber trail across the water.

I hadn't fished since the summer I was ten, the last
summer Dad took Joanna and me out in the rowboat at
the cottage on Pamlico Sound. I felt important in my orange cotton life vest and happy that Joanna, though older,

had to wear one too. Dad would push us off from shore, Mom still sleeping in the dark, and then we'd be out in the mist, just the three of us, hunkered down with our poles and lines. My secret pact with myself was that I'd never be the one to speak first: my insurance that the day would last, that when we went back to Charleston at week's end Dad would stay for the remainder of the summer.

Dad was always the one to break the silence in that boat. He'd start to hum, then sing, everything from hymns to marching songs to old Cole Porter tunes, mixing up the words or pretending to forget till Jo or I corrected him.

We'd come back to the cottage in the late afternoon, sticky with Coppertone, salt water filigreeing our hands and arms and legs, cooled by the bay and by the memory of the bay. Mom and Dad together would slit and gut and cook the fish, and I'd be careful to do whatever seemed necessary to sustain all the good feeling.

In the canoe, I pulled Vivien's salmon booklet from my back pocket. It said that when the salmon are born, they follow the lake's rim to the riverhead, then swim the current to the sea. In the ocean, they swim deep and low, for two years, circling the Davis Strait, the coast of Labrador. What, precisely, they do up there remains a mystery. Maybe they just eat, and grow.

I've always wondered how the salmon return: if there's a magnetic compass lodged in their brains, or if they navigate celestially. But it's true what you hear: they find the same river from which they came and splash back up, propelling themselves against the current, a great wash of fish against water, until they come to the very spot where they spawned out.

I trailed the bobber across the lake's still membrane, not so much wanting to kill a fish, not really interested in all that gutting, but wanting to feel it alive in the boat with me.

When I started reeling it in, the fish was slapping and twisting against the boat, sudden, alive. I finally got both my palms around its wet scales and smoothed its slippery and scrabbly skin. I could feel it breathing the air, the air that would soon cause its expiration. I stared at the fish head-on, both of us panting, the hook firmly pricked into its gaping mouth. I could feel its heart beating against my palms.

I pulled out the hook and slithered the fish back into the water, watching it turn luminescent in the lake, then disappear like a tendril of smoke into air.

SIGHTING

When I rounded the shoreline's bend and saw the riverhead feeding into the lake, I had no idea what I'd find next: this island was so different from anything southern and familiar that I realized, then, that I'd ceased to make comparisons. The lake water was simply itself, singular and inky blue, reminding me of nothing I'd seen before.

I drew the paddle back into the ink and pulled the nose of the canoe around into the freshet. The water snaked toward me, forcing me to dig and dig in order to make any progress at all against the current. But I kept going; I got it into my head that I had to make it up the stream, past that pine branch that dipped across the swale, then past that rock ledge jutting out. I had to keep jaying the paddle around to keep on course, and forward. The water, despite its hurry, was quiet, and I could hear the wind shiver the leaves every now and then, or the call from a kingfisher diving ahead of me.

I admit that I was tired when I saw the motion between the trees, and I was concentrating on the water, not the wooded trails around it, so I could be wrong, but there, suddenly, I thought I saw a splash of animal color, different from the texture and the vibrancy of the green leaves, the rocks, the tree bark. A flash of tawny brown, in between the pines, a swift catlike motion, then gone.

My breath caught in a cry in my throat, but I don't know what I would have called out had my voice functioned. Maybe, just, "Animal!" But as it was, I pulled on the paddle, and pulled some more, craning and dodging my line of sight right, then left, then right, but I couldn't keep the animal's hide in view.

Around me, the woods had gone silent, more silent than before; even the kingfisher was gone.

I let the current push my boat backward, as if it were a tiny birchbark canoe like the ones Dad brought me and Joanna from one of his trips. I laid the paddle across my knees, and put on my sweatshirt, suddenly cold, and rode the canoe in the current back to the lake's wide path, the water like a cartridge spilled open in a green bowl.

M O T H S

Most evenings that summer I stayed at the cottage. I'd cook some meat on the grill—they call that "barbecue" up here—and eat on the porch in my jeans and the old sweatshirt I'd borrowed from Pat months before I left. I still felt bad about not returning it, but it gave me a slim rope tethering me to her, to my other friends, to the life I'd vacated.

By August I was starting to miss Pat, and Taylor, and some of the places of North Carolina. But I wasn't ready to go back, and I even started thinking that maybe I never would; maybe that part of my life was, simply, done.

At night after I ate and before I'd go into the water, I'd sit on my porch in the light from the kerosene lamp, and watch the lake gradually sink to darkness, while the boat lights came on. The moths would hit against the porch screens lightly, tapping the thin wire, and I could hear the lake buffeting the rocks down by the shore. I liked opening my eyes as wide as I could, and imagining the pool of memory in my head being flooded by the lake.

From the porch of the cottage next door I could hear voices, the soft summer voices of people who know each other well, laughing together and retelling old and well understood jokes, and I longed for the company of my pals back in Durham. I could hear them, but the white pines and brake of laurels formed a shield and I couldn't see the other cottage; in fact, once the island went dark my entire range of vision was limited to the black of the porch screen, broken by the white frame, and beyond that the closest trees, softened in the lantern light. The porch was an entity unto itself; it seemed its own little island on the island, the dark pressing against the screens, the lantern light, me in the one red wicker chair, isolated, obscured, and safe.

But some nights I grew restless, or if I was out already at Vivien's I didn't want to go home to the cottage. Nights when I knew my image of the lake flooding out the pictures wouldn't be enough, and I'd have to be mobile in order to outdistance them.

One night I had dinner over at Vivien's, and we watched the sky stay light. I wondered aloud if the darkness took so long to descend because we're surrounded by water, or because we're so far north, and it wasn't until after I spoke that I realized with relief that I didn't, for a moment, remember the reason.

After the last strip of lavender slipped into the lake, I

got in my car and backed down Vivien's long driveway, and drove past the meadows around her house, the grasses all gray and trembling in the night wind.

I turned on the Quebecois radio station. As I approached the drive for my cottage, I realized I had to keep going, and I did.

I wasn't thinking of vanishing again, but driving by my own place gave me that good feeling, that I'm not bound to anything or anyone, that none of us is, really; that I could just drive by my own place and keep going, into the night, up Route 10 and onto the ferry to Canada.

"I'm just passing through," I'd say to the border guards, and they'd believe me, because I have such an honest face.

But that night I stayed on the island. I drove past my cottage and over to the cape that reaches west, and as I crested the hill, the Quebec piano playing, the cool summer air rushing in my open window, I saw in the sky one brilliant explosion of red and blue, a single, random fireworks display, utterly out of place this August night. Well, I thought, and I thought it must be some kind of sign—one of those damn signs that I never know how to interpret, like the day I found a tiny key, to a padlock or a very old cupboard door, lying on the sidewalk at my feet.

When I pulled in the drive to my cottage that night, I was glad I'd left on the little light that rests in its milky-white cup above the kitchen sink. From outside, the cottage looked sweet and homey with the light on, and I felt cared for, even if only by myself.

As I walked up the pathway to the door, I saw that the light was filtered by spots, by hundreds of moths that had gathered at the single lit window and covered the screen.

I slipped in the door. The moths had slipped in too— they'd nestled their way around the old, ill-fitting screen, and now they covered the walls and floated in the soapy dishwater I'd left in the sink. One side of the old curved re frigerator was covered with their moving, twitching wings.

I just wanted to drop right there, I suddenly felt so tired, the old tired that I'd thought would drain my blood all last winter. I was tired of trying to forget, and tired of doing everything alone, of figuring wondrous signs by my-self, of sitting on my porch and watching night descend alone, of single-handedly controlling the arthropod popula-tion in this cottage.

But I'm good at this kind of thing. I got out the fly-swatter and decoyed the moths with the light into the bath-room, where they'd be contained, unable to escape.

They were easy to kill. I knew they would be, because they're the same kind that hover around my bedside lamp while I'm reading in the bed that countless summer visitors have slept in, propped up against the pillows, listening to the lake.

I learned soon after moving in that if I brushed my hand, or the spine of my book, against one of the moths it would succumb, leaving just a charcoal trace across the white pillowcase.

D I V I N G

Sitting on my porch one evening, after a day of scrubbing down Bill Withers' boat, I laughed out loud to think that I hadn't put it together about amnesia and immersion in water.

After all, in all my diving at the lab at Beaufort I'd seen enough cases of nitrogen narcosis to know that a deep plunge into water can also plunge a person into another reality. So it stands to reason that that reality could be the one I longed for, with the slate of memory blank as the aphotic water.

Rapture of the deep, it's called. A diver plunges to the depths, the blood filling with nitrogen, and then the brain extinguishes some synapses, some ability to separate this from that. Self from non-self, maybe. It's like we're called back to our origins, to the deep beginnings of evolution, the watery amniotic sac, afloat in the womb, afloat in some new dimension.

One time I dove with a graduate student down to the beautiful wreck of the *Carib Queen* on a search for delicate arrow crabs. When we hit ninety feet, he took off his mask and looked at me. I'll never forget the look on his face: his eyes wide, perplexed, and at the same time happier than I'd ever seen him. A little confused, as if wondering what he was doing in such a terrestrially adapted body. And then he just waved and swam off, gliding away from me into the dark water.

I chased after him, and caught his arm and dragged him up against the pressure of the depths; he didn't resist, but in that last moment, that moment we catapulted from the depth that made him go narcotic to the depth that brought his senses back, his face filled with sadness, like the sadness of a child who has been told a terrible truth about the world. He looked so sad that I wanted to just pull him back down, let him go.

Outside the porch, the fireflies flicked on and off, on and off, and across the lake, a few lights on the boats began to glow.

Later, Dave said he couldn't remember any of the narcosis, but he always referred to that dive as our best. I'd ask him what was so good about it, and he couldn't tell me; it wasn't the samples we'd collected, or the clear blue sky, or the dinner we'd all had later to celebrate someone's breakthrough in her research on mollusks. But he'd often say, "Remember that trip in April, the wonderful one?"

"The one where you got narked?" I'd ask.

"Was that the same trip? April eleventh, I think it was. It was the best dive we ever made."

When he talked about it, I'd look closely, and his eyes would hold just a trace, a shadowy smudge, of that happiness he'd felt, that amnestic rapture of forgetting.

On the porch, I scratched a match into flame, lit the citronella candle in the galvanized tub. Night was now pleated all around the island. Below the porch, I could hear the water, insistent, breaking on the shale.

PARTY

I'd been afraid it would catch up to me—the past, I mean, the life I'd vacated. How could it not?

When I lived in Durham, I'd seen most of my acquaintances move on; they'd get another degree or change careers or meet someone in Arizona, and move on.

Before I vanished, I liked thinking about the people I knew fanned out across the country, people I'd lost touch with, and even people I'd never known very well. I liked thinking of the whole web of who I knew, or who knew someone I knew, casting a big net over the United States of America.

But now, here, on this island, I felt severed, and I liked it. I didn't let myself think of the people I'd known. Instead, I'd lie in the narrow bed that came with the cottage and think of the water moving out there. I took to opening the six-paned window that faced the lake before I went to bed, so while I slept I could hear the water and the fluttering wings of the bats that lived in the rock ledges.

Of course, memory kept tugging at me, and my personality kept surfacing, more now with Vivien inviting me over for supper every week, and our long, winding conversations on her wooden steps that led down to the water.

When she had the party, and I went, I knew I had to be prepared.

I was standing in Vivien's kitchen feigning a consuming interest in the view from the window above her huge old porcelain sink (why had I accepted her invitation? Was I really so human that I bent that easily to loneliness?) when I heard the woman's voice approaching from the hallway. Immediately I recognized the tone, that lilt-sink-lilt that would call me home in the very hour of my death, that unmistakable voice of the eastern fields of North Carolina.

First I was thrilled: Someone's found me! But then I was stunned, and whispered "damn" under my breath. I had to think fast.

When Vivien came into the kitchen, I was relieved that I didn't recognize the woman with her. Vivien introduced us.

"Pleased to meet you," we said almost simultaneously, and with almost the same voice. We both laughed.

"Your voice—you must be from North Carolina," she said, and I could see she was happy to have found someone else from so far away.

I was prepared. "I lived there briefly, once. But you

should know, I'm amnesiac, and I really don't recall a thing from back then, and it's very difficult for me to try."

I was banking on the probability that she'd suffered the same damn training in intensive politeness and gentility that had inoculated me against being nosy or forward. I was right.

She looked startled, but quickly covered for herself. "I'm so sorry to hear," she said. "Don't you just love Vivien's house?" She stepped ahead of me into the dining room, bright with the light reflecting from the lake, and then onto the porch. I was afraid she'd say more, somehow try to maneuver the conversation southward. But I also wanted to hear her talk, to hear that familiar reach of vowel and consonantal slide.

Luckily, she also had that southern propensity for revealing the details of her own life, and once I asked her what brought her all this way, she kept going on her own. I let the sound of her voice play over me, while I leaned on Vivien's porch rail, looking out to the water.

NEWTON

Sometimes at night I'd lie in my bed at the cottage, the window to the lake open, listening to the waves splash against the shale. Sometimes I'd think about Newton's laws, or the laws of thermodynamics, and I found them oddly comforting.

In high school, I would cut English class and gym, and show up late most days. Mom was so preoccupied with Dad's various escapades or with her own vague symptoms that she wouldn't notice, and would write me notes even as she admonished me to get my education so I wouldn't end up like her, stuck. But I usually showed up for chem and physics and biology. I didn't understand why everyone wasn't just wandering around slack-jawed at the theories. Sometimes it was hard to take notes, because I'd be too astounded to write.

At night, when I'd hear Mom and Dad fighting down-stairs, or when the silence of Dad's absence would stretch into the early hours, I'd think of what Mr. Stilson or Miss Farnham had said that day in class, and play out the theo-ries, imagining the speed of sound or my heart opening and closing in my chest as the headlights of passing cars shone intermittently into my room.

Here, it was the same. I liked lying in the bed, listening to the water, thinking about how the molecules of a wave don't move forward, but rather around in a square, always in the same place. Or how everything is always falling to chaos, how the more energy that's lost the more the chaos builds.

And hadn't I proved Newton's first law since leaving Durham? A body at rest tends to remain at rest; a body in motion tends to continue in motion.

But then what about the third law—that every action has an equal and opposite reaction? This would imply that there was some reaction to my departure. What would be equal? What opposite?

At night, when I started thinking like that, sometimes I'd have to turn on the lamp by the bed, and switch every-thing from the chaos of dark back to its usual semblance of order. Sometimes I'd get up, go into the big room, sit in the mission rocker, and rock to comfort myself.

To go to sleep, I'd think about my favorite law: that matter is neither created nor destroyed. I'd try to prove it wrong: What about the newborn baby, an eggshell, or a storm? Or death, atomic bombs? Still, even the driftwood fire I light on the beach makes heat, and heat is real. Or even the bodies of raccoons I've seen on the island roads will wash into the lake, molecules assimilating into milfoil that waves up from the depths.

Maybe, I'd think, walking back into the bedroom and sliding in between the sheets, maybe nothing in me was created by Libby. Maybe she didn't create my love for clean lines in a room, or my depth of wonder at shifts of light. And maybe, then, nothing in me was destroyed when she left. Maybe I came to her as she came to me—as whole, intact, as when she left. Changed, yes: sometimes with her I could feel my electrons and protons speeding up, spinning faster and faster around their nuclei as we'd argue politics or toss a boomerang out and watch it hurtle back or stand beneath the wind's tug on the kite. But me—the essential me she loved—that me was the same as before we met. The same me as after.

SPEAKING

The rain started as speckles blistering the lake's skin—
pock, pock, pock—and then, as Vivien and I took the first
big spoonfuls of cold ice cream, the drops started simultaneously coming faster and disintegrating into a misty near-
rain. We were sitting on her front porch in the deep wicker
chairs; she'd just brought the butter-pecan ice cream out to
the wrought-iron table.

Outside, the birds quieted down and the earth started
emitting that fresh rainy summer smell. We sat in our
chairs, our feet resting on the porch rail.

Somehow Vivien got onto the subject of libraries and
research. How she liked the tall rows of shelves in the library in her Vermont hometown, a perfectly round stone
building, "no bigger than this house," with its old pine card

catalog and parquet floor, the cheap shellacked pine shelves and the corkboard with notices pinned to it by the door.

Most of all, she'd loved the reference books in that library—just one long shelf with a big *Random House Dictionary* and a line of *Encyclopaedia Britannica* and an *Atlas of the Americas*. On top of the shelf sat a globe, and next to that Vivien's favorite, a celestial globe.

"I loved looking through the plastic, through the constellations, as if I were up in heaven. I'd sit there and turn the knob to make the moon go around the earth and the earth spin around the sun. When I was in the seventh grade, Jimmy Richards broke that knob; I still remember the remarkable disappointment I felt from then on. I didn't want to go to the library much after that—it made me too sad to see the incapacitated solar system, just sitting there, unmendable."

I sucked a chunk of ice cream with a big pecan in it off the silver spoon, then worked at sucking all the ice cream off the pecan. I was hoping that somehow this subject would change, or at least shift before we got too much more into the delights of research.

"Of course, now I'm over it. Now I love going to the library on the mainland. Have you been there? They have everything: all the important dictionaries, the best maps; I could spend hours there just looking up bits of trivial information."

She looked at me, over the rim of her bowl, expectantly, her brown eyes comforting, like the eyes of a young black bear, soft.

To my horror, I heard my voice saying, "I had a friend once who loved research so much she took extra hours at work so she could look up such things as what the mean temperature in Australia is or how many members the National Association of Agoraphobics has.

"She always had some new reference work to show me. On holidays, she'd dig out the *Dictionary of Customs and Rituals,* or sometimes she'd look up psychiatric diagnoses of our friends." My breath was coming faster, and I could feel my heart lumping in my chest, but I couldn't stop myself. I tightened my double-fisted grip on the ice cream bowl. "We always talked about making a historical dictionary of scientific terms, illustrated and cross-referenced, so you could look up, say, optic nerve, and see not only what it was but when it was discovered. One time she made me a blueberry pie in honor of February, which she'd discovered was Pie Month and Canned Food Month, both." Vivien was smiling, and leaning forward, as if ready to catch me, as if I were about to fall.

I took a breath, then let it out with a sigh. "Well," I said, trying to hold back the galloping tremble in my voice which was threatening to crack, trying to regain whatever semblance of composure I'd possessed. "That was a long time ago."

I didn't linger that evening; I told Vivien I had some letters to write. Back at the cottage, the rain was still misting up the air around me, but the setting sun was breaking through, making the lake and the lilac bushes and the bobbing heads of the tiger lilies all a little luminescent, the grass nearly transparent, like Easter cellophane. It all looked like one of those black-and-white photos with the pastel colors painted in.

I swam a long time that night, about halfway to the headlands and then back, my shoreline rising in interrupted visual takes, lifting like the high ground in a dream.

SALVAGE

The only noise was my breath, familiar, rasping and scratching through the oxygen hoses, then out in a cluster of bubbles. My air—the air that had just made a complete circuit of my vessels, transformed to pockets rising from the depths.

Maybe Isaac Newton was right. Maybe matter *is* neither created nor destroyed, but just cycles back, looping over in another form.

Meanwhile, I scrubbed at the sailboat's hull with the scraper. Through my goggles, I could make out just enough to see my progress: the boat's hull whiter where I'd been, white as a whale's huge underbelly, while the hull I had yet to move across lay barnacled and slick with milfoil and algae, almost indistinguishable from the murky water.

Underwater, with a task at hand that required thought

as well as physical exertion, I felt pretty safe. My body adopted that near weightlessness, that feeling that my veins were ballooning open, countered only by my tank and the iron plumbs that hung along my waist.

What was underwater moved into sharper focus, and everything of the land slipped dreamier.

DREAM

At the end of the summer I had the dream. I was in the canoe, then swimming, and from the water I could see the shore, and on the shore, an animal: not the mountain lion of California or the bobcat that's adapted to humanity so well, not even the disappearing jaguarundi of the southwestern desert, but the single most mysterious beast of the Northeast: catamount.

In my dream, she was lolling on the rock ledge shoreline, and I was swimming. I wasn't afraid, but I wasn't ready to go on land yet, either. The catamount stood, and stretched, and looked out to the water, then dove in and swam to where I floated in the inky blue.

Then I woke up.

All summer I'd heard talk of the catamount, most of it discounting the people who said they'd seen one.

One time at Ray's Feed and Antiques, where I'd stopped in to pick up some wax for the canoe, he was talking with a customer about the catamount.

"This woman, I don't know where from, said she saw one out on Milo Point. Swore it up and down," Ray said, leaning one elbow on the old cash register. I pretended to be terribly interested in the squares of color on a paint chart, afraid they'd stop the conversation if they knew I wanted to hear.

"Well, far as I know, they still haven't got any evidence," the customer said. I'd seen her around the island. She was about fifty, and had her gray hair neatly curled in ringlets around her head.

"They say they can't make a positive identification until they find proof, like a photograph or a skull or something," Ray said.

"Well, that gal who saw something at Milo Point, didn't she find a paw print?"

I wanted to step in then, and say, "Paw print?! Paw print's good enough for me," but I held back.

"So she says. But I guess by the time the Fish and Wildlife people got there, some kids had come by on their dirt bikes."

Ray and the woman then started going on about the kids and their dirt bikes, how they'd be the end of life on the island as they knew it, and I brought the wax over and paid for it.

"Be careful of the catamount," Ray called after me as he handed me my change, winking.

SUIT

I'd been thinking a lot about skin all summer: some days I'd
lie in the sun by the water listening to the quiet lake waves,
thinking about how my muscles and blood are just floating
around in this sac, like the larval monarch butterfly that
disintegrates, then completely reorganizes its cells in the
cocoon: transmogrification.

By late summer I still felt fragile, but sometimes I'd be
flooded with joy, or gratitude. One evening I paddled the
canoe over by Vivien's bay, and there, in the dusk, saw a deer
bending its head down to drink, and I couldn't imagine
wanting to be anywhere else.

Maybe the amnesia exercises were helping. And finding this life, forming this life on the island.

Vivien helped too, even though I didn't see her that

much, with that steady way of hers, her brown eyes looking right into my face, unblinking. Sometimes she'd cook me dinner from her garden, and we'd eat on the wooden steps that led down to the water, and wonder together at how seeds and dirt and light could produce these snap beans and tomatoes.

The evening that she told me about the suit, the lake was going lavender and blue in the twilight. "This is the beginning of the autumn sunsets," she said. We sat on her steps, a bunch of Concord grapes in a wooden bowl between us. She'd brought out a couple of bulky wool sweaters from the attic, and the cedar scent drifted up, mingling with the scent of browning leaves.

Vivien leaned back with her elbows on the step above her, and said that when she was about my age she'd seen a suit—a silky blue gabardine—on a mannequin in the window of a secondhand store in Manhattan, where she lived then. She walked in, tried it on, and it fit her perfectly. The sleeves' edges just grazed her wrists, the pants were long and loose, and miraculously, given her small waist and narrow shoulders, the jacket fit too.

"When I tried it on, I just felt—different. More real," she said, her hand fluttering, fingers stiffening and then relaxing in the air the way they do when she gets excited talking.

She said she brought the suit home, feeling the weight of it like a heavy secret in the bag. She put it on, with her nice white shirt under the jacket and a thin red tie, and walked out to the avenue to hail a cab.

"I just threw my arm in the air, and the first taxi

stopped," she said, looking surprised the way she must have looked there, the New York City air bright and crowded around her.

She went to the Metropolitan Museum of Art, and clipped the museum pin on her lapel. She walked around, her hands in her deep pockets, standing for a long time in front of the painting of Joan of Arc, looking for the angels

Later, she rode the subway to an uptown restaurant, and followed the maître d' to a window table, then sat quite contentedly alone, not even reading her *Times,* just having her meal, in her suit.

From my spot on her steps the lake sounded calm; I could smell the autumn smells, and I listened, rapt, watching her fluttering hands, as she gave me that sideways look as if calculating my reaction. It was thrilling, deeply thrilling, to think of Vivien—Vivien!—in that suit, confident, sure that a taxi would stop, that the maître d' would take her to a good table, that no one would block her view at the museum.

She isn't timid, but there's something awkwardly charming about her interactions with the world, and I was sorry in a way to think of her shedding that the day she wore the suit. Ordinarily, she seems a little out of place, so confident with her short hair and firm stance combined with that fluidity she has. That shy persistence.

What I didn't tell Vivien, but what I thought, was how odd it seemed that in my vanishing—in my total abandonment of my former life—it hadn't occurred to me to crossdress, to slip even farther by slipping into a fictive man.

I think in some ways I could pull it off better than

Vivien. My breasts are smaller, and my hips are narrower, especially after all the weight I lost last spring.

But on the other hand, it makes sense that I assumed my new identity would be female. My own mother never knew how to fit in; she was always going around in jeans and an old sweatshirt when everyone else's mother was wearing one of those shirtdresses with little flowers on them. Maybe she didn't care, or maybe she figured that everyone was looking askance at her anyway: what does it matter how the wife of the town ne'er-do-well dresses? It had taken years of training myself, of studying women's magazines and making careful observations of cousins and co-workers, to be able to slip into the masses of women, and become what people expect a girl to look like. To pass.

I didn't tell all that to Vivien, of course, because she didn't know about the vanishing. I'd told her more than I'd told anyone here, but even she didn't know about the awards I'd gotten from the science academy, or what the me who'd vanished had loved deeply: coffee steamed with milk, the southern shore of the Atlantic Ocean, watching spring warblers through the round binocular lenses, a woman named Libby. I hadn't told Vivien about the amnesia exercises, how each time I woke with the nightmare on my tongue I'd dive or swim into the water, even in late summer, with the water so cold it hurts.

Now I think of the depth of the lake water, the few loons that float there, the herons and how they disappeared in September. Or now, Vivien in her suit, walking up those wide, welcoming museum steps, her pointy shoes clicking and scuffing on the smooth stone.

That evening I suddenly wanted it to be all right for her to wear her suit, and for me to wear my black dress, and for us to walk together through the doors of an uptown New York restaurant, but I know she'd be too self-conscious for that. I know she can only wear her suit when she's alone, just as I wait until dark before I go down to the rocky shore, undress, and slide into the smooth cold water.

Vivien said the best part of her day in the suit was when she got home. She loved the familiar click of her key in the lock, and loved how her cat came and wound around the gabardine pant legs. She loosened her thin tie, took off the jacket, and pushed up the sleeves of her white shirt.

The very best part, she told me, leaning forward, her hand fluttering onto my shoulder as a breeze lifted from the lake and whispered across our faces, the very best part was when she lay back in her bathtub that night, the suit hanging from the hook on the bathroom door, her skin all smoothed with the soap, her body wavy and mysterious under the water.

AUTUMN

Slowly the island emptied of summer visitors, vacationers sifting out and leaving just the year-round residents, the true islanders. Evenings started spreading earlier across the water, the sunsets glowing bluer and more lavender each night. One morning I woke, stepped onto the porch, and saw that frost had covered the pines and grass, making the island shimmer.

Libby had tried to teach me to observe the seasons as they merged from summer into early fall, from winter into spring, but every year it happened too fast. We'd have contests to determine who would see the first tinge of yellow along a single leaf on the maple in our yard. She was fascinated with the cusps of things, with anything teetering on the verge of change.

But I spent too much time looking down to see the colors turn. Or, even as I'd be walking or driving to the lab at Duke, I'd be thinking of the water, of the ocean floor. Invariably, it was Libby who left the first soft gold or crimson leaves on the kitchen table.

On the island, I saw the change, maybe because it was so gradual, or maybe because now I had to find it for myself.

Each tree around the cottage went through its transmutation at a slightly different pace; even the white pines seemed to transform.

The lake water got rougher, and it started to shine a deeper and deeper blue. I finished cleaning the boat hulls for Bill Withers, and he sailed out for Florida, leaving me with a good chunk of money, and work to last into the late fall, sanding and painting his schooner and patching his canoes.

The trees, this far north, scuttled their leaves much earlier than they did in Durham, or even back in Charleston. Still, the effect was much the same, the green grass giving way to yellow, then to brown, as the leaves dropped and scattered.

One day I drove by Sandy's Snack Shack and saw two young men in jeans and sweatshirts nailing wide sheets of plywood across the windows.

The next week, I pulled onto the road to drive to the ferry and came up behind a little shortened yellow school bus, short like a miniature loaf of bread.

At Ray's store I bought two postcards from the rack, with pictures of the island taken from a low-flying propeller plane, the green of the meadows and blue of the water so faded that the island could have been nearly anywhere, and later that week I sent one card to Pat, the other to Joanna. "I'm okay," I wrote. "I'll be in touch."

I still dove in the water evenings, or walked straight in, or canoed out to the middle of the lake and hung my head backward over the gunwales. I'd given up trying to forget, because I didn't have to work at it anymore.

Instead, I started wondering what effect my disappearance had in Durham: Had Libby come back to the house, opened the boxes, sold my things? Maybe she had come back, and was waiting for me there, keeping my study vacuumed. Maybe she'd retrieved my things from the attic, rescued them from their boxes, and put everything back around the house.

Or maybe she had come back, tugging Doris in her wake.

Now, what difference did it make?

BAT

It was late October when Vivien came by the cottage. When I first heard her knock on the wooden door, I figured it was her, and then I was startled, guilty that I hadn't even thought it might be Libby.

When Vivien stepped inside, I realized no one had ever been in the cottage with me before. I was glad I'd just washed my dishes and had shaken out the floral-print rugs the day before. Vivien sat on one of the kitchen chairs, her knees wide apart, leaning the chair back on its hind legs. She looked like a canid, a wolf or coyote, with her graying hair and sharp features.

"You can't stay here much longer," she said, and I got scared. What else would I do?

"It's going to be too cold in another month. The water will freeze, and listen, this place isn't even insulated."

"Oh," I said, still not sure what her point was.

"So, I want you to come stay in my place for the winter. I'll be leaving next week for Albuquerque—these winters are getting to be too much for me. Doc Wells says I need some dry heat for the winter months."

I didn't know what to say. I hadn't really been thinking about what I'd do when the cottage got too cold. I guess that all this time I'd really been thinking that Libby would somehow, miraculously, come find me. That I'd be back in Durham by winter.

"That would be super," I managed to say, but I could feel my voice coming out stilted. What if I missed Vivien? My god, what if I'd grown attached to Vivien and would miss her?

"Great. Come by the house in the next couple of days, and I'll show you where everything is," she said, standing, and then she was out the door and gone. I looked around the cottage. It looked a little different, bigger, emptier, than it had before.

Vivien gave me a long list of instructions: how to put up the storm windows, how to fix the pump if it broke down, who to call in case of plumbing troubles. The usual, all written out in her tiny, neat letters.

"Be sure not to stay in the cottage after it's too cold," she said.

Once she left, I was afraid I wouldn't know when it was too cold. What's too cold, after all? And wasn't cold proving to be pretty good to me?

But one morning in early November, I knew it was too cold when I woke with something soft in my hand. I didn't know, at first, what it was—I could feel it moving a little under my fingertips.

When I looked, and saw it was a bat, at first I was afraid; but then I remembered that I had nothing to fear anymore. It was panting a little, and I looked closely at its doggy, pinched face, at its soft brown fur, at its wings lying neatly folded against its sides.

I gathered this bat into my hand and brought it close to my cheek, wondering at the softness of the fur, awed to think that it had somehow found me. Maybe it was some kind of messenger: a messenger from Libby? Maybe she's looking for me? The old thoughts came clicking in, even as I knew this bat was just a bat, and I nearly laughed out loud at the thought that Libby would come for me now.

This bat just blew in looking for a warm winter roost, a place to hang and drop its pulse and breath rate until spring.

MOVING IN

I didn't have much packing to do. All my clothes fit back into the two striped bags I'd taken from Durham, except a couple of heavy sweaters Vivien had lent me. I packed a box of other things I'd collected since moving into the cottage: a fossil I'd found down by the water, the faint impression of some ancient hoof, some post-therapsid foot that landed on the shore eons before I did; the paintbrush and little book of heavy paper and the tiny square of paints I'd bought at the stationer's; the rose-patterned cotton cloth I'd bought for the porch table. I left the stiff-spined journal under the bed.

As I packed my food into a couple of paper bags, the boxes of macaroni and cheese and the cans of New England clam chowder, the odd compendium of edibles that had never appealed to me, or that at least had no affiliation with my former life, seemed to shed their mystery, their magic ability to help me erase myself. I put the bags and the box into the back of the Chevy, which stood like a gracious steed, waiting.

When I looked around the cottage once more, I was surprised at how little I'd changed the place; I'd just passed through, like the lake breezes rustling over the floral chaise cushions and the white curtains in the windows. I saw the page I'd torn from *Wescott and Williamson's* still tacked to the wall, and left it there.

Ray met me at the cottage, pulling his pickup onto the lawn that was now yellow and speckled with red and orange leaves. A few stalwart late flowers still shot forth their reckless blooms.

"Finally moving out, eh?" Ray said, clambering out of the pickup, smiling. He looked rough and weathered, like Vivien.

"Vivien said not to stay after it got too cold," I said, feeling that I should explain my decision to move. "Thanks for coming down to help me."

"I've helped Viv board this place up since she moved here. Wouldn't seem like fall without it."

We didn't say much else that afternoon, beyond the words necessary for piecing together the puzzle chinks of board and window. I held the wood flush against the windows while Ray banged the nails into the frames.

When we put the last board up, over the door, I felt relieved, as if something had been boarded up in that cottage, something that needed dark and solitude for the winter, along with the amnesiac's journal and the page on amnesia and the soft brown bat that had made a home hanging from the pole in the bedroom closet.

T E L E S C O P E

Dad would have loved this night sky, I thought as I stood by the lakeshore shortly after moving into Vivien's. The air was cold, but I didn't mind.

Above me, the black sky was littered with stars, looking clearer, more precise than I'd ever seen them. The constellations seemed huge, a giant Orion chasing a mammoth Taurus across the dome, Taurus' horns tipping far into space.

I sat on one of the big rocks by the shore. In the still lake water, I could just make out the reflection of the stars.

The summer I turned ten, Dad took me and Joanna camping in the Smokies. That sky had been like this one, with so many stars it made me dizzy to look up. There, by our tents pitched in a field, Dad gave me my birthday present.

When I first saw it I thought, despite its size, that it must be what I had been wanting more than anything: a jewelry box like Joanna's, with tiny drawers that pulled out and a secret compartment for the really special things and a ballerina that popped up and twirled around to "Swan Lake."

I was scared as I opened the box by the campfire, because I could tell by how excited Dad looked that it wasn't a jewelry box.

It was a telescope, child-size but, as Dad said, "not a toy."

"Wow," I said. "I had no idea." Joanna shot me a look as if to say, "Don't hurt his feelings."

I tore the box open in what I hoped approximated genuine excitement. "This is great, Dad."

He set it up on a flat rock a little ways from the campfire, then adjusted the lenses for me. I tilted my neck back and peered in, and there was Mars burning red and real, a real planet, not just a dot of brightness in the night sky. "Wow," I said again, this time with a little more enthusiasm.

Later, I lay in my sleeping bag and thought about how he couldn't have possibly known about the jewelry box: he hadn't been home enough to know how I longed for Joanna's. Stupid, stupid, stupid, I said to myself, then curled onto my side, and thought about the animals out there around our tents, animals who don't care about jewelry boxes or telescopes.

I only used that telescope a couple of times, when Dad would tell me there was some astronomical wonder scheduled to appear in the sky. The last time, there was a trine of three planets, and Dad set the scope up in the backyard, even though by then the lights from the growing city of Charleston were so bright that it was hard to see. While I dutifully squinted into the telescope, I realized Dad, standing near me, was crying, trying to catch his breath back. I stared into that telescope until my neck hurt, until I was sure he'd gone into the house, and after that he didn't take the telescope out anymore.

But still, sitting on this rock with such a splashy display of stars, not just above me but duplicated in the water, too, I wished I knew where he was now, wished I could invite him here.

I shivered; the night wind was picking up. Just when I was about to cross the lawn toward the house, I saw a shimmer of light jettison across the sky, almost like a searchlight beam. I kept looking, and another light blended in with the first, following it. The aurora borealis, pulsating over the pole and then radiating down here, to the island.

PAW PRINT

When I saw the first paw print, I thought it was dog. But the second one stopped me dead in my tracks, right there on the dirt path that leads from Vivien's back porch into the woods to Mount Venteux.

The second print, and the third, were unmistakable, huge cat-paw tracks in the mud of the trail softened by the Indian summer sun. I crouched down and peered into the print, the four smaller pads like a corona over the large central pad. I sniffed the air and tried to smell a catamount nearby, but all I could smell was the woodsmoke coming from the fire I'd left burning at Vivien's. I took a few steps forward, a few to each side, but there were just the three prints. I knew that later the mud would freeze up in the cooling fall air. The tracks would probably still be good tomorrow morning, but I didn't want to call anyone to report this.

Instead, I walked back down the trail to Vivien's, and searched through her books on mammals until I found *Great Cats of North America.* After dinner, I sat on the living room couch, the fire warm in the stove, reading about the catamount.

The book was old, printed in 1952, and the glue that held the pages to the spine was dry and cracked, so that I had to be careful not to let the pages slip out.

It said that catamounts roamed the northeastern corner of North America, these mountainsides and woods, taking down deer and the occasional moose, feeding on rabbit and squirrel in the lean winters, denning up in rock cliffs or along the sturdy branches of the wide trees.

The book said the last catamount around here had been bagged in Maine in 1938, then hauled off to the University of Manitoba for dissection.

There was a picture, one of those paintings you find in old books like that, of a catamount lazing along the branch of a pine, thick tail dangling from the limb, its face staring placidly, steadily at the painter. The colors were muted, the dark green of the boughs and the biscuit of the cat, so that the whole thing looked dreamy and real at the same time. I turned the page, and there was another painting, close in, of a catamount making its kill, bringing a deer down into the snow, all instinct and no remorse, the blood along the deer's nape and its terrible horrified eyes, the scene caught in that sanctified moment just before the kill.

I stood, and checked on the fire. When I shut out the lights in the living room, the outside plunged into brightness, the arcing moon reflecting off the icy frost that painted everything. I stood at Vivien's window, looking out over the long lawn, but no animals appeared.

GOLDENEYES

I'd just sat down at Vivien's white metal table that looks out over her porch, just lifted one of the delicate teacups painted with tiny roses to my mouth, when I saw the ducks land on the lake.

Vivien's view of the lake is wider than the one I'd gotten accustomed to in the cottage. Her porch spreads across the front of the house, and then the lawn slopes down, grassy and green all summer, now yellowed and splotched with leaves from the maples and the birch. Beneath the lawn, the blue expanse of water pulls taut out to the horizon.

I was sitting at that table, thinking about nothing in particular, when I saw the few ducks—maybe about five or six—land on the water, sudden, unannounced. I gasped a little, and stared, not wanting to move for fear they'd take off again, but not wanting to sit still and only see them hedged through the glass window and the porch rails.

I put the teacup down in the saucer, then slowly pushed the straight-backed chair back, rose, walked to the porch door, opened it and went onto the porch. Outside, the morning air was cold, and I could see that a thin layer of frost had limned the bushes, the grass, the trees, all of it luminescent in the morning light.

And then, before I really had a chance to take in the ducks that had settled on the water, a tiny line of black appeared in the sky, small enough at first for me to think it was just some miscellaneous protein in the gel of my eye, but then enlarging, gathering momentum and mass, until the tiny dots became ducks, a whole gathering squawking flock of them, black-and-white ducks filling the sky, circling above the lake, circling closer, tacking back, lowering, lowering, until they scudded in two lines onto the water.

I counted them in patches, the way I'd learned in those first wildlife classes; in the end, I counted over two hundred, right there, quacking, paddling, living ducks covering the belly of water in front of Vivien's house.

Leaning against the porch rail, I watched them for a long time, first listening to their squawks become less and less frequent, then go silent together. After a little while, they started diving; first one disappeared into the water, then another, and another; then one up, another down, another up. "Up, down, down, up, up, down," Libby and I had said to each other, laughing, while we watched the buffleheads in Minnesota so many summers ago.

The ducks stayed that whole month in Vivien's little cove, warmed by the rivulet that fed down through the meadows.

Evenings, after working on Withers' boat, I took to sitting on the single wicker porch chair that I hadn't put out in the barn for the winter, wrapped in Libby's old blue sweater and my gray sweatpants and heavy socks, just to watch the ducks. I'd rest my feet on the porch rail, elbows on my knees, prop Vivien's big professional binoculars up to my eyes, and stare at the ducks. That first evening, after supper, I sat on Vivien's brown cordurory couch looking through her old *Audubon Water Bird Guide*. How about a Labrador duck? As soon as I saw the little painting of the Labrador, I thought, Yes, that's it. And then I read the description, my blood pounding faster through my mammalian veins. It all fit—but imagine a duck flying in, landing on this lake water, all the way from Labrador. I stood, and in the lamplight combed through the high bookshelves lining one wall of Vivien's living room; I hauled down the big dusty *Atlas of the Americas;* Labrador wasn't that far from the island, after all. Back to Audubon, and the terrible words: "extinct since the early 1900s."

How could this be true? Look at Labrador, the pink boundary lines a little faded in the atlas, the land all bifurcated by the arteries of lakes and rivers. Think of Tunungayualuk Island and Saglek Bay: surely there must be room up there for a few stalwart surviving Labrador ducks?

But no: "this type of exploitation during summer when

the birds were flightless so reduced the bird population of that area that the trips became unprofitable."

No. I felt that pulling in my chest, and I rubbed the map a little with my finger. How could they be gone, just like that? Like the great auk gangplanked into eternity. Imagine: the "structure of the Labrador's bill shows that it was adapted for sifting out small objects and suggests that the bird's feeding habits may have been unique among sea-ducks."

But no more; the Labrador's been gone for years, no longer nestling its spotted eggs in the northernmost rock crevices. Another duck knocked out of the world of evolutionary possibilities by its fine feathers and thick oil. Another mystery, unknown diet and family system, another beast relegated to obscurity.

Finally I narrowed down the ducks that had settled in front of Vivien's to either common or Barrow's goldeneye. A couple of times, I wished there were someone I could ask, but I wanted to figure it out for myself. In Vivien's basement, I found an old telescope, like the one Dad had given me, and I set it up at the window.

Alone, here, I reveled in my detective work, narrowing the possibilities, discarding some ducks, considering others, combing Vivien's books for information on how ducks live—even with that relentless image of the summer rock-bound Labrador, protecting her nest of doomed eggs as the hunters approached.

I learned that despite their appearance of thorough incompetence in flight, ducks migrate along the north-south corridors tremendous distances, putting in the minimum amount of work necessary to achieve the best possible habitat. I learned how the waterfowl expanded in the Eocene, splitting into the families and tribes: Anatidae, Alcidae Merginae. Imagine the skies along those routes clouding up with blue-winged teal, mergansers, or going white with the wings of snow geese.

And then one morning in early November, I bent over Vivien's rosebushes, pruning them back as she'd instructed me. The ducks dove and rose, dove and rose near me on the lake, until I took a few steps too close to them, and heard a wild pattering of webbed feet on water; I looked, and they were rising off the lake, rising all in one group, as if of one feathered body, and the air filled with the sound of their whistling wings, a sound never replicated on this earth, a whirring, humming, like no sound caused by any other duck or bird or goose, the sound of common goldeneye precisely as described in the books.

I let the branch I was pruning hang in my hand and stood there listening, just listening until all I could hear was the little splash of the lake waves, waves now empty of common goldeneye.

Does the water miss the goldeneye when they heave into the northern air? Does it remember the whistling?

The Labrador duck swam with the gray gadwall in brackish waters, feeding on small shellfish and maybe seeds. I wondered, sitting huddled in the single wicker chair, if the gadwall misses the Labrador, even now, nearly a century after the last Labrador was wrested from its rock crevice nest. Is there some genetic memory of gadwall that waits for that flock of black and white, the soft feathers, unique scoop-shaped bill sculpted by evolution's brilliant errors?

MUSEUM

The ferryboat thunked to a stop at the mainland dock, jig-
gling the passengers: the old woman in a gray wool coat, the
two teenage girls who had studiously applied their makeup
as soon as we left the island, the man with his young daughter. We all woke up a little, and then paraded down the
steps and followed the cars off the gangplank.

I was glad I'd left the Chevy back at the island: I liked
the feeling of walking under the bare trees, now emptied of
their yellow and orange leaves. Besides, I was here on a mission, and I felt determined and brave to be walking.

I'd memorized the directions, and turned left, then
right. I passed the stationer's, the hairdresser's, and turned
right onto a wide street, Bouchet Boulevard, and there it
was: the Northeastern Museum of Natural History.

It was a big building for this city, a small building by most museum standards, but it had the appropriate wide marble steps and iron banisters leading up to the heavy wood front doors.

I stepped inside, and breathed in the heavy, heady scent of all those stuffed and mounted creatures, all that dust, that sheer accumulation of curiosity piqued and satisfied and piqued again.

I walked into the main hall, the Hall of Northeastern Mammals, thinking, I guess this is where I belong now. The hall had the usual mounts, a beaver, a porcupine, and the skeletons of possum and of rabbit. I walked along the rows of displays, the beaded hats sold by the Indians or stolen by the settlers, the old hand-tinted photos of the islands before the cars and the telephone lines.

At the end of the hall, I stopped. There, in a glass case, stood the largest cat I'd ever seen, standing rigid, its head in a perpetual tilt, huge front paws nearly crossing in its step forward, all biscuity brown except for the black nose of its rounded face and the black tip of its long, heavy tail. The sign said: "Catamount."

"Miss Didelphis?" I jumped; I hadn't known anyone was that close to me. I turned, and there stood an old man, his white hair clumping out around his head like a puffin's tufts, his mustache and beard neatly clipped.

"Sorry, yes," I said, putting my hand out. He took it, and held it for a moment rather than really shaking it, and looked me in the eye.

"Charles LaFountain," he said. "I see you've met our prized resident—the last one shot in these parts; as a matter of fact, it was shot out on your island. But you didn't come to talk about fabled big cats, did you?"

I wanted to say, "Hold on, let's talk cats," but he was mesmerizing, and clearly in charge, propelling me back across the hallway I'd traversed, unlocking a door and leading me up a narrow stair, keeping up a constant chatter all the while.

"When you called, you said you were interested in marine life, and we certainly could use your help, but unfortunately we don't have much of a marine collection here. With your expertise I'm almost embarrassed to say it, but where we really need help is in the relabeling of the bird collection."

"Well, I . . ."

"Now, here we are," he went on, opening another door and leading me into a room lined with high metal specimen cases. He unlatched the door to one, and before I could offer my help, he hefted the door down, propped it against a case, and pulled out a drawer.

The birds lay in neat rows, a brilliant array of feathers, each with a fading tag on one foot. He slipped a pair of reading glasses from his breast pocket, then lifted one of the birds as carefully as if it were still alive.

"See, this tag is so old the data is nearly obliterated. It's quite a job. How are you at reading inscrutable handwriting?" he asked, peering over his glasses at me and smiling for the first time.

I laughed out loud. "I used to get letters that I had to spend hours deciphering," I said, still laughing, and he started to laugh too.

"So did I. During the war my paramour, I suppose you'd say, wrote me faithfully, but sometimes I could make out only the salutation and the sign-off," he said. "Then again, sometimes that was all that mattered."

"It's a good thing you knew your own name, or you wouldn't have known who they were to," I said, and we laughed again.

We stood there, laughing in the specimen room, Charles LaFountain cradling that bird as gently as if it were still alive. I was laughing about Libby's handwriting, laughing and I knew it, laughing and suddenly happy to be right where I was, with my past just as it was, and my present, present.

BELIEF

The stuffed catamount I'd seen in the Hall of Northeastern Mammals was the last one shot "in these parts," but not the last one seen, or so Charles LaFountain told me in the big workroom back in the ornithology collection as I rewrote the specimen tags.

He had his own work, too. He was methodically going through the old letters the collection had received, all of which were organized by date, and reorganizing them by subject. "Every time I get some inquiry about some historical fact, I have to dig through everything, and I won't always be around to remember it all," he said.

He was compiling the file on the catamount while we worked.

"You know, there are so many sightings and reports since our mascot was shot that even this old skeptic is nearly convinced," he said. "But nothing definite has been documented."

"You mean a lot of people have seen them?" I was trying to write as small as I possibly could, but I still couldn't match the tidy letters on the original tags.

"Oh sure. There are accounts of everything from a young guy in the 1930s to a middle-aged lady who said last summer she saw one out to Milo Point, out on your island," he said.

I looked up. "I heard about that one."

"Well, too bad she didn't have a camera." He passed a letter to me with a black-and-white photograph clipped to the back. It was dim, and blurry, but the image of the animal crossing a snowy dirt road was unmistakably catlike.

I handed it back to him. It took a few extra seconds, because his hands shook so badly that he had to try a couple of times to grab it. "But Charles, doesn't it seem a little unlikely that one would be on the island? I mean, how would it get across? I haven't run into any catamounts riding the ferryboat."

He laughed, and picked up a file folder marked "Correspondence, 1954–55." "No, dear, they'd swim across where the water's narrowest, up by the point. And of course, in winter, they'd just walk."

"Walk?" I was starting to worry; he must be ninety. Maybe the whole catamount business is a delusion, I thought.

"Across the *ice*, dear," he said.

"Oh." We worked quietly then.

Maybe extinction is like amnesia, I thought. Maybe we allow ourselves to forget the tawny fur, the heavy tail and wide-splayed paws, until one early morning we wake and remember the feel, the sight, the scent of catamount.

DEER

I thought at first it was a big pile of leaves, blown or pushed into a heap by the side of the path. The woods were decaying now, and cold; nearly all the leaves had fallen to the forest floor, layering over the other years' leafmeal. Everything in the woods felt damp, and some of the trees had an icy sheen along their trunks.

I walked closer to the leaves, then stopped, and stared, and suddenly I could see that what I'd found wasn't just leaves, but was also animal, the shape of the deer's head puzzling out from the shapes of leaves, the way the drawing of the old woman reveals itself within the drawing of the young woman. First the deer head, and then a hoof, another hoof and leg. The bulk of it had been covered over with leaves, and I could see now that whatever had done the covcring had dug deep down into the leaf floor; the leaves were wet, soaked through, and black with mold and deer blood.

I looked at the eyes of the deer, and the eyes looked not back at me, but off someplace, glossy and blank.

Then I saw the evidence: the paw print imploded into the mud of the path.

I stepped away from the dead deer as quietly as I could, and back to the path. I'd read about how the catamount eats what it can, then hides the rest of the kill, only to return days later for another feed. The cat's prints led up the hill, away from the house, and I turned downhill, my legs all watery and weak.

Sometimes I would see them as if in a parade, all these animals that in my lifetime are walking off extinction's gangplank: catamount at the lead, the jaguarundi and the northern swift fox not far behind, slinking along on their well-oiled joints; the Louisiana black bear and the wood bison, hanging their shaggy heads; the key deer and the Columbian white-tailed deer, picking their way along on their dangerous high-heeled hooves. I would see them all sometimes, at night, just before I fell asleep: at the end of the parade, the black-footed ferret, the spotted salamander, and the American crocodile, plodding splay-footed and heavy-jawed, and above them all, the silent whirling of the piping plover and the whooping crane, the whippoorwill and the roseate tern. I'd see them moving, defeated, toward extinction's close horizon.

I used to imagine them walking away, leaving the forests and the beaches empty and silent except for some starlings and a few field mice. But now, as I lay in Vivien's bed, I thought about the reversal of extinction, and I imagined them coming back from the precipice, the ducks quacking in excitement and joy, the wood bison trampling ahead, the deer clattering up the rocky hillsides, necklaces of delicate evening primrose and the Heller's blazing star that once covered the Blue Ridge Mountains strung around their necks, and above them, the skies filling with the riotous relief of birdsong.

That night, I imagined the catamount in the woods near Vivien's house, pawing down the hill, nosing its kill, then nestling in some strong pine branches to sleep. I imagined it looking from its perch out over the woods and meadows, over the cold lake, the frosted lawn and house, seeing the light in my bedroom suddenly go out.

FERRYBOAT

By early December I'd gotten accustomed to riding the
ferry back and forth, to living on the island, to being called
"Virginia." I found that I liked the cold, liked waking in the
morning to the frost skinning the windows, how the wood
spat and steamed when I laid it on the fire. I wasn't even
trying to forget anymore, but found myself simply missing
Pat, and Joanna, and even those things about myself I used
to love but had abandoned in my quest for amnesia.

One night I drove up the mainland gangplank of the
ferry to go home. I got out of my car, the cold wind bluster-
ing all around me. The other drivers and passengers,
padded in down and wool, stayed in their warm cars, but I
climbed up the metal stairs to the lookout deck where I
could see everything.

The engines started up with their grind and whir, and

just as the kids on the gangplank reached down to hook the chain across, a woman came running down from the ticket booth, her leather jacket open, a big red and black scarf blowing around her neck. She was slowed a little by the big canvas bag slung over one shoulder, but still she made it, and leapt over the chain and onto the boat's deck.

I watched all this from my post at the railing. I thought she looked like Libby. She had that same awkward grace, that big way of moving her rangy arms and legs. That boy-ish quality, as if she just wanted to be on the ball field all the time.

The ferry pulled away from the dock, the water slap-ping against the metal. I thought about how different this ferry is: like the ferry to Okracoke, it's really two boats back to back, each like a cross section of a boat, each side with a set of controls and a big glowing compass, one for going east and one for going west. But this ferry, this northern boat, had an icebreaker on either prow, and the little cabin in the middle up top, with the wooden benches and list of safety instructions, was heated, and the steam crept up around the windows as we made our way across the lake.

I stood there, outside the cabin, and wondered if Libby would ever be gone from me. I didn't think of her so much anymore; I'd even missed the anniversary of our first kiss, not noticing until a week later that it had gone past.

Standing on the deck that night, I thought about the other things, the territory of my life with her I hadn't wanted to traverse: the times that she'd be hurt, or mad, and slam out of our house, and not come back for days. How the terror that she'd be gone for good would rivet me to the window all night. How something that I'd done or said would balloon up in her mind, generating catastrophe with every breath she took. The times she thought I'd lied, and how she'd say, "But how can I ever trust you?" How much like Dad she'd been, after all, both of them chased by some terror of their own; how I'd responded to her in kind, predictable in retrospect.

I thought about how Libby had loved photography because she loved stopping the motion of time; how she'd loved the shadowgraphs of high-speed photos, where really the image finally imprinted on the paper is just a shadow of the object, not the object itself. I remembered standing with her in the darkroom, the acid stop bath searing my nostrils, as we'd watch the image gradually wash up onto the paper.

It had felt like magic to me, and like magic the way she'd bend her knees a little in the excitement of seeing the image appear. But standing there on the ferry, I wondered at how she could love something so still; I wondered if maybe she hadn't loved her own image of the world—and of me—more than she'd loved the world—and me—in all our wonderful, fallible contradictions.

In the end, maybe I'd been lucky—lucky!—to have felt so much love, to have been exposed on the cliffs of the heart, and to have lived through it. Lucky to have been able to leave it, to find this island, this ferryboat, my own re-creation of the world.

I stood on the deck a long time, and watched the lights

of the mainland recede into a tiny strip of white, then vanish. I tilted my head back, and above me the Big Dipper and Cassiopeia and the Pleiades listed slowly across the sky.

I heard the cabin door slam open, then shut, and felt next to me the presence of the woman who'd blown late onto the ferry. She stood a little distance away, and looked up. She'd zipped up her jacket and wound her scarf around her collar. "Do you know the constellations?" she said with a whisper of a Quebecois accent, smiling and turning toward me.

Up close, she didn't look that much like Libby after all. In fact, maybe the resemblance had just been something else—the wind, or something.

"I know some of them," I said.

"Do you live on the island?" she asked.

I nodded.

"How did you ever find it? I mean, what made you move to so remote a place?"

"Sometimes I think I invented it," I said, laughing. "I just needed to escape a few things."

"I wish I could do that. You are so fortunate. On the other hand, I must return to Montreal, to the big city."

"See that constellation?" I pointed into the speckled night sky, to the glinting group like a brand on the shoulder of Taurus. "That's my favorite, the Pleiades."

We stood staring up into the sky, the wind cold against my face, the stars above us fractured into bits of light, the bright spine of disarticulated night.

C A T A M O U N T

I wasn't even paying attention to the shoreline when it happened; I was crouched down by the water, looking out over the lake for ducks, hoping the last of the goldeneye hadn't flown south yet. The cold wind was chapping my face, and I knew I should have worn more than Vivien's old sweater and checkered black and red jacket.

Then I felt something near me, something alive. That snap of twig, leaf-rustle. I turned, expecting to see a junco fly up from the branches of the short pine, but instead, standing on the shoreline, a few feet away, there it was: catamount.

It was unmistakable, the tawny fur, the heavy black-tipped tail that was so weighted it dragged a little, shuffling the leaves that had fallen on the lawn. It was lithe and tall, and so close to me that we could have touched had I taken two steps. I could see everything: the white whiskers trembling a little, the rounded ears, a pink scratch running across its black nose. I could hear it breathing, see the puffs of warm air from its nostrils.

I somehow remembered that you should stand, so you don't look like prey. As I rose, the cat let out a noise that set my heart kicking, at first, because I thought it would be the catamount scream. But it made a catlike throaty cry of curiosity, looking at me with those intelligent black eyes, and tilted its head a little to one side. Then it pivoted, and walked into the green pines and bare white birches.

I watched it slip between the trees, and away, all sinewy muscle, lean flank.

That's when my legs went weak and my head felt filled with air. I sat down on the ground. So it was true: the catamount had battled back from the edge of extinction, just as I had propelled myself back from the cusp of amnesia. My god, I'd nearly obliterated myself, that untamable nature. I knew I would tell no one about this encounter. Keeping the catamount secret was necessary not only for its survival, but for my own.

When I could stand, I made a quick survey, and plucked a clump of tawny fur from the low pine. It was thick, and soft. I let it float into the rivulet that feeds the lake, then stomped along the shoreline, pressing down on the wide feline tracks with my boots.

I walked back to the house across the lawn, the changed lawn. Everything felt different, now: stoking up the woodstove, cooking my dinner, turning back the feather comforter on the bed.

Out there, the catamount, following deer paths, nosing in the dead leaves, walking heavily across the night island, beneath the sky's night mouth and its wide constellations, safe, like me, at last.

FIRST SNOW

It was gradual, the way the lake froze. I had been preparing myself for a sudden freeze, for waking one morning to lift the lace curtain in Vivien's upstairs bedroom and see the frozen expanse spreading out before me like tundra. I'd thought that when the lake froze solid, all the way across, when I could see the icehouse lights blink on in the dusky afternoon, when the waves against the shore were silenced, then Libby would be gone from me. Then I'd be able to breathe.

But as it turned out, it wasn't nearly that dramatic. It was just that one afternoon in mid-December I was sitting on Vivien's corduroy sofa, looking at one of her heavy art books—baroque paintings, I think—and I looked up to see that the clouds were bundling up across the sky, whiter than any clouds I'd seen before. Back in North Carolina, the

clouds would ride in sooty gray, or black, dunderheads glowering their warnings: Get off the beach! One time at Okracoke Libby and I hadn't heeded them. Let's stay, let's stay and watch, she'd said, and I'd agreed. Yes. We scrambled up into the dunes, made a tent of towels and the plaid cotton spread. We crouched together, witness to the lightning rift in the dark sky, the waves spraying and rocking harder against the sand.

But here, on this northern day, the clouds darkened the sky even though they looked so white, to the point where I couldn't make out much of the pictures in the book. As I stood to switch on the lamp, I saw the snow beginning to drift down, drifting tiny white dots, spinning from the clouds to cover the lawn and lake.

I flicked on the lamp, then stood in the porch doorway, watching the lawn and dark, smooth water gradually turn white. The water absorbed the white snow at first, then just let it settle on the carapace, till the whole lake was covered.

Except for one curving, winding path of dark water, winding from the big boulder near the apple tree and out into the lake. I watched while the lawn, the bare bushes, the pines, all sank beneath the white, and still that one strip remained, dark and wet, slippery like a Möbius strip of cellophane against the snow.

I put on Vivien's barn jacket and a woolen cap, pulled on the rain boots I'd gotten on the mainland, and made my way through the snow down to the water's edge. My boots slid a little on the snow, and I couldn't see very far ahead, but when I got to the lake, I realized the dark snake of water was where the current flowed: some underground

spring must seep up here, and the current runs out, out, deep into the lake.

Maybe Libby will never be completely frozen out of me, I thought, and then I felt relieved that I no longer had to work at this, so relieved that I lay down, supine in the snow, letting it drift onto me, wetting my face and hands, as if I could become part of the island landscape, accustomed to snow and the aurora borealis echoing its light behind the clouds.

The next morning I woke in the white bedroom, the morning light brighter than I'd seen before. I propped myself up and lay in the warm nest of covers just looking out the windows, out to the sky so blue that I thought this bed could be floating underwater, under a bright Caribbean wave.

I got out of bed, and pushed aside the lace curtain. The snaking rivulet still wended out from the shore, but it was narrower. Everything else was white, and very still.

I could just make out the curving margin of the shoreline, and a little closer to the house, the shadow I'd made with my body, which now looked like the impression of an angel, an angel who'd fallen to the earth, wings still moving.